Mortar and Pestilence

A Kay Wellington Cozy Mystery

Melissa Plantz

FIRE and GRACE
Publishing, LLC

FIRE & GRACE Publishing, LLC

For My Mother-in-Law,
Jean
With Love Always

Contents

Chapter 1

Kay and the Ring of Fire

The last thing I wanted to do on a Monday morning was give Mr. Padasky suggestions for relieving his "ring of fire," a side effect from his Hepatitis C medication. But, then again, the poor frail man, who had known me since I was a tiny tyke, was in some agonizing pain.

I took a deep breath. I loved my job, working for my father in his pharmacy for the last twelve years in our small town. But sometimes, the demands of the job wore me out. I pushed my glasses further up my nose and tucked a loose strand of raven-black hair behind my ear. "Mr. Padasky, that medication, Incivek, is a slightly older Hep C med, and if you don't eat at least 20 grams of fat with every dose, then the medication will irritate the lining around your...." I trailed off as I discreetly made a circle with my index finger.

The line behind Mr. Padasky at Wellington's Pharmacy grew by the minute. And the citizens of Locklyn, North Carolina, could be a bit nosy - something that I was more than aware of.

The hard-of-hearing Mr. Padasky leaned forward. "The specialty pharmacy explained that to me. I need something to cool it off, Kay!" The man bellowed into my face.

"Of course, Mr. Padasky, follow me," I answered, smiling at the gentleman and ignoring the wide-eyed looks from the other customers. Then, just when I didn't think the morning could get any worse, I spotted Lydia McKellan standing in line.

"Kay! Tell James I'm here to see him," Lydia shouted, referring to the full-time pharmacist on the phone, who also happened to be Lydia's ex-husband.

I managed a smile in the woman's direction, careful not to make eye contact with her anymore. Lydia was the worst. No doubt, she was beautiful with her platinum blonde hair and 5 foot 11 height. But everyone in Locklyn knew the real story.

Lydia McKellan was evil.

She'd divorced James. The sweetest man in the entire town. James was soft-spoken and polite - except when it came to Lydia. She drained him dry with alimony, and for some reason, unbeknownst to anyone, James still had her covered on his health insurance. My father, Thomas, the owner, and manager of Wellington's Pharmacy, had once divulged that Lydia received as much as forty percent of James' income.

I ran over to the pharmacy counter where James stood with the phone up to his ear, his dark brown eyes focused on the computer screen in front of him.

"James, Lydia is here and wants to talk to you," I whispered.

James rolled his eyes. "What does Pestilence want now? Tell her I'm broke."

I hesitated. Did he really want me to say that in front of the other five customers in line and a very uncomfortable Mr. Padasky?

"No, don't tell her that." He sighed. "I'll be done in a few minutes. On the phone with an insurance company!" he yelled through the plexiglass to Lydia, who only shook her head as she took a seat in the waiting area.

I led Mr. Padasky to the hemorrhoidal products and pointed out some cooling pads he could use until he felt better.

"Thank you, dear," Mr. Padasky announced loudly after I'd rung him up at the register, the other customers looking impatiently in my direction. "You are the best pharmacy tech I've ever seen. I'm glad your Pa kept you." He turned to regard Lydia, who sat in a chair, tapping her foot and sending dagger eyes to James' face. I was thankful for the plexiglass.

"Stay sweet, Kay," said Mr, Padasky. "Or, you'll wind up a mean old bitty who no one wants to stay married to like *some* people."

The line of customers snickered at Mr. Padasky's insinuation, but Lydia was too self-absorbed to notice that the insult was for her benefit.

As I waited on each customer quickly, James came out from behind the counter to speak with Lydia, motioning her to the consultation room. However, the she-devil found it easier to share her business with everyone within hearing distance.

"This. I need this filled immediately," she barked to James, handing him a prescription bottle.

"Are you serious, Lydia? You had me come out here for a refill of Claritin? It's over the counter. Aisle Three. Get it yourself."

"No, I will not. I called the insurance company, and although it is an OTC, they will pay for it again. One hundred percent. So fill it."

James' jaw clenched. "You could have just given it to Kay."

"Why? So she can mess it up?"

My cheeks heated as I tried my best to pretend I couldn't hear the conversation four feet from the register.

"Kay's been a pharmacy tech for over twelve years. Longer than I've been a pharmacist. She's not going to mess up your Claritin. I'll fill it, but it will take at least thirty minutes. I'm busy today." James stormed back around the counter and slammed the bottle down near the computer.

"I don't have time to wait, James. I haven't been feeling well."

"Then come back tomorrow."

Lydia crossed her arms over her chest as she eyed James, then turned her Medusa eyes on me. I held my breath, my body stiffening into a statue. She looked me up and down.

"Better yet, I want it delivered. Today."

James sighed. "You want a bottle of Claritin delivered to the house? Why don't you grab a bottle off the shelf, and *I'll* pay for it?"

Stubbornly, Lydia shook her head. "No. Refill the med and have Kay deliver it to me this afternoon at the house. I'm sure she can at least do that. Bye, Love." She threw her hand in the air for a half-hearted wave.

And with that, Pestilence left the building.

"I 'm sorry about this, Kay," James said as he stapled the bag containing Lydia's Claritin closed. "You know how she is."

I sighed as I slid a bottle of lorazepam back on the organized shelf, each label meticulously facing out. "I know, James. It's okay. I don't mind. I'll probably take my lunch right after I leave your house. I mean *her* house," I stammered. The McKellans had only been divorced a year, and I still wasn't used to it. James had given Lydia the house and moved into an apartment on the other side of town.

"Sounds good. Take your time. With Miranda here now, we should be fine."

Miranda Good was the other tech that worked for my father's small pharmacy. Everyone knew that the redhead with the pixie cut and nosering had a massive crush on the young pharmacist.

"I can't believe you just didn't tell Lydia *absolutely not* about the Claritin, James," Miranda said as she popped a Gobstopper from her smock pocket into her mouth.

"It's not that easy, Miranda. Lydia doesn't take no for an answer."

"That's because you haven't made her listen. I bet if you stood up to her, she would stop all this ridiculousness."

James frowned and ran his hand through his blond hair. "Just let it be, Miranda. And stop tossing Gobstoppers into your mouth from your pocket. It's unsanitary. Not to mention, you're going to break your teeth."

Miranda rolled her green eyes. "You don't seem to have a problem telling *me* no."

James half-grinned at us before turning his attention to a row of prescriptions needing his approval. "Go on, Kay. Pestilence awaits you."

"Pestilence? You must mean Lydia. I saw her on the security camera," my father said from the other side of the pharmacy counter.

"And you wisely stayed hidden, Thomas," James answered.

Thomas Wellington laughed, his round belly moving up and down. "I've known Lydia since she was a teenager, James. I told you then, and I'm telling you now. That girl's a nightmare."

James muttered under his breath, then spoke louder, "She wants Kay to hand deliver her medicine today."

Before my father could ramble off some remark about always serving the customer, I jumped in, "It's for *Claritin*, Dad."

Thomas laughed. "She's still a customer, Kay. Just drop it off, then take a long lunch."

"Oh, I plan to. That is if I still have any appetite left."

I drove through the wrought-iron gate of James' old subdivision. Dad and I had been here a few times when James still lived at home. He'd invited the employees over for summer barbeques and Christmas parties. Lydia's house was the third one on the right and could easily house my place twice over.

Of course, unlike Lydia, my house was paid for - I'd inherited my grandparents' home, and since my parents already owned their place free and clear, the two-bedroom one-bath house with the big fenced-in backyard on Lanier Lane fell to me. For all I knew, James could still be paying the mortgage on Lydia's house too. What did Lydia have over on James to make him fork out so much for her expenses?

Considering that Lydia acted like a witch most of the time, I surmised it was some sort of a spell.

I pulled my Trailblazer into the driveway and willed myself to get out of the truck and take the prescription bag to Lydia. I was really hoping to keep the confrontation to a minimum. I only wanted to drop the bag off and pick up my lunch.

I stepped onto the porch of the brick split-level home. Such a large house for one person. The McKellans didn't have any children, probably for the best. With a sigh, I rang the doorbell and waited. Then rang it again.

Was Lydia not home? I stepped down from the porch and peeked into the two-car garage. Lydia's little Fiat was parked inside, but there was no sign of the woman herself.

I frowned. Should I leave the bag in the mailbox? Or inside the screen door? No, that would be irresponsible. Instead, I decided to walk around the back deck and knock on the sliding glass doors leading to the dining room. The backyard was quiet, with only the hum from the in-ground pool making any noise.

"Lydia? Are you home? It's Kay from the pharmacy."

"Kay?"

I turned to see Mr. Padasky leaning over the fence separating the McKellan's property from his. "Hey, Mr. Padasky, I forgot you live next door to Lydia."

"Yeah, it's a privilege," he answered sarcastically.

"Is she home? I'm supposed to drop something off to her."

"Who knows? She and that boyfriend of hers are always up partying with friends through the night and sleeping in late. I was surprised to see her at the drugstore this morning."

"Hmm." I knocked on the glass door again, a little louder this time.

"She's probably catching up on her beauty sleep," Mr. Padasky sneered. "She and Eben had a knock-down drag-out fight last night."

"Eben? Is that her boyfriend?"

"Yes, and a poor excuse for one. Nothing like ole James."

I tried to peer in through the blinds into the dining room but couldn't make anything out. I pulled my cell phone from my back pocket. "Maybe I should try to call her. I think I still have the number from when James lived here."

"Well, if you don't get an answer, try the back door. Sometimes she leaves it unlocked." Mr. Padasky started to turn from the fence.

"Thanks. How do you know she leaves it unlocked?" I asked, listening to the ringing sound through my cell.

The older man shrugged. "She told me once when her mail was delivered to my mailbox by mistake. She said if it happened again, just leave the mail on the kitchen counter. Of course, I've never done it. I just send it back to the post office."

I saved my eye-rolling for after Mr. Padasky retreated into his house and instead tried to call Lydia one last time.

L ydia didn't answer.

Would it really hurt anything if I just opened the back door and set her bag on the kitchen counter? Maybe the woman was in the shower washing the evil out of her hair and couldn't hear me. Surely, Medusa had to sanitize her snakes now and again.

I moved off the deck and rounded the sunburst-designed railings to the white wooden back door with one vertical window. I knocked on the narrow pane of glass one last time.

"Lydia?" I called as I poked my head into the kitchen. Then I allowed the door to swing open wider. The kitchen didn't look anything like it had when James and Lydia had been married: the marble countertops were filled with bags and papers, white cabinet doors hung open, the silverware drawer was pulled out, and the plastic trashcan was knocked over, fresh trash flowing freely on the tile floor.

"Lydia?" I called again, a bit of uneasiness creeping into my voice. Had there been a struggle? Mr. Padasky had remarked that Lydia and her new boyfriend, Eben fought. Was this from last night?

I slid a heavy plastic grocery bag filled with canned food across the counter and dropped the pharmacy bag in its place. Although my brain rejected my next idea, my body moved toward the dining room.

Maybe I should check on Lydia. Maybe this guy Eben wasn't a good guy like James. At least, Mr. Padasky seemed to think so.

The dining room was pristine; I figured it was because Lydia probably never used it. I made my way into the formal living room, which was also empty and neat. I stopped before a framed picture of Lydia with her fashion model good looks. I was older than her by a few years since I was fresh into thirty, well, thirty-three, but Lydia held a look out of her eyes that seemed older. As if she'd seen things.

Where else could I check? I knew there were a couple of guest bedrooms on this floor and a bathroom, but the family room and the Owner's bedroom suite were downstairs.

"Lydia?" My voice trembled as I descended the stairs. "Are you home?"

My hand trailed down the bannister as I crept closer to the bottom step. The house was eerily quiet. When my hand touched something sticky on the newel post, I gasped and withdrew it. My fingers were covered in a sticky red substance. Carefully, I brought my hand close to my face. The metallic scent pushed my stomach into my throat, but I forced the bile back down.

Lydia was in trouble. I made the decision. I would peek into the family room and then leave the house quickly and call James. He would know what to do. He would call Lydia and make sure she was safe somewhere. If this was blood - and by this point, I was pretty sure it was - James would probably want to call the police if he couldn't locate his ex-wife.

However, when I poked my head around the door frame, all my plans flew out the window.

Lydia lay on the thickly carpeted floor, part of her head bashed in and bone fragments sticking out. The pool of blood under her head and body had soaked into the white carpet, making it appear as if Lydia had died in the snow.

She didn't just keel over dead, Kay! Someone did this to her.

With that last thought, I sprinted up the stairs and out the front door to Mr. Padasky's front porch and banged on his door. The last thing I wanted to do on a Monday morning was stand in a dead woman's house with a killer on the loose.

Chapter 2

Black Coffee with a Splash of Courage

The following two hours were a blur. Mr. Padasky listened to me and then called the police. In shock, I scrubbed my hands, dialed the pharmacy phone number, and calmly told my father about Lydia. James arrived shortly after. The police were next door at the crime scene; however, they had asked me to remain at Mr. Padasky's until they could get my official statement.

James slumped beside me on the worn couch, holding his head in his hands. "She told me she hadn't been feeling well. I thought she was just being dramatic. I thought she was just being Lydia," he insisted through tears that threatened to fall any moment.

"Here, James, drink this," Mr. Padasky shoved a stoneware mug at James' face. "It's some black coffee with just a splash of courage."

"You put alcohol in his coffee?" I asked shock clearly on my face. The older man never ceased to amaze me.

"Of course, Kay. The police are going to want to question him."

James' eyes grew wide. "But, I was at work. Ask anyone."

Mr. Padasky made a "hmph" sound in his throat. "You think that matters? James, you are too nice. You let that little girl walk all over you. It's men like you that get the blame for something like this."

I frowned. "That's ridiculous, Mr. Padasky. No one is going to blame James for Lydia's death. I worked with him all morning."

"Miss Wellington?" A deep voice carried from the doorway into the living room. A tall, well-built man dressed in a suit and tie stood just under the archway.

I immediately stood. "That's me," I said, crossing the room. I stopped a few feet away from him. It was hard to make eye contact with him. He was, well, celebrity-crush handsome. I ignored the feeling of something stirring inside me, something long buried. "I'm Kay Wellington," I offered, looking up into his chocolate-brown eyes.

"Miss Wellington, I'm Detective Pierce Cornell with the Locklyn Police Department," he said, reaching for my hand. "We're investigating the suspicious death of Lydia McKellan."

"Where's the other guy?" Mr. Padasky demanded as he made his way over to us.

"The other guy?"

"That other detective I see around town. What's his name, Kay? Graham something? The one marrying the Reynolds girl."

I nodded. "Alec Graham. I see him at the pharmacy now and again."

Detective Cornell ran a hand through his thick brown hair. "Detective Graham is on vacation with his fiancee in South Carolina this week. I'm lead detective on this case."

"Huh," Mr. Padasky answered, looking the detective up and down. "Then where's the girl?"

"What girl?" I suspected Detective Cornell was beginning to lose his patience.

"The female detective."

"Detective Anita Wallace transferred out to Seattle. *I'm* here now. I take it you are George Padasky?"

"As I live and breathe," the older man said. "Lived in this town all my life. Know just about all the families."

Detective Cornell nodded, then shifted his gaze over my shoulder. "So, that makes you James McKellan, Lydia's ex-husband."

James stood, and I watched as he slid his trembling hands into his trouser pockets. Mr. Padasky had probably scared the life right out of him.

"I am, but I haven't seen or talked to Lydia since this morning. And that was in front of an entire store full of customers."

"I'm not accusing you of anything, Mr. McKellan. I'm just working out what happened to your ex-wife." Detective Cornell met my stare again. "Miss Wellington, may I ask you a few questions privately? Perhaps on the front porch?"

"Of course." The detective motioned for me to go ahead of him to the front door, but he paused, his hand above my head, holding the storm door open.

"Mr. McKellan, I'm going to request that you remain here until I am done with Miss Wellington," he said loud enough for his "suggestion" to be heard through the house.

"No problem. But I didn't have anything to do with this," James answered.

"It's procedure to question the spouse or ex-spouse, in your case." Detective Cornell's eyes remained on the door.

I heard Mr. Padasky let out a gruff laugh. "Told you, boy! You're in deep trouble!"

"Surely, you don't think James had anything to do with this, do you?" I asked the detective with the slightest five o'clock shadow starting to form on his face. "James was at the pharmacy all day. He never left. A half-dozen customers saw him."

Detective Cornell took a deep breath as he shut the front door to Mr. Padasky's house. "As I told you, Miss Wellington, it's standard procedure to question the ex-husband." He motioned for me to sit in one of the white rocking chairs lining Mr. Padasky's porch.

I sat down heavily in one, listening to the creaking wood. "Mr. Padasky probably doesn't use these often. Not since his wife died a few years ago."

"He lives alone?" Detective Cornell asked as he lowered himself into another rocker and maneuvered it across from me.

I nodded. "His health is getting worse."

"Seems like he is a bit cantankerous." He smiled.

I smiled back like a goober. What was wrong with me? I was over thirty years old. Much too old to be acting like a schoolgirl with a crush.

"What can you tell me about Lydia McKellan? And why exactly were you here, Miss Wellington?"

"Please, call me Kay. Everyone does. Except sometimes my father. He'll call me Katherine. I was named after my grandmother." I pressed my lips together to make the word vomit stop. Why was I so nervous?

Detective Cornell smiled again. "All right, Kay."

I told Detective Cornell about Lydia demanding that I bring her medication to her home this afternoon. Then about finding her on the family room floor.

"What made you go looking for her in the house? From the way you made it sound, there wasn't any love between you and the victim."

I leaned back in the chair. "Well, I didn't hate her. I didn't *like* her, but I didn't hate her. I went looking for Lydia when I saw the state of her kitchen. It appeared that something happened in there."

"You think there was a struggle? Between Ms. McKellan and who?"

"I'm not sure, but Mr. Padasky said she and her boyfriend fought last night. You'll have to ask him."

A commotion on the lawn next door suddenly grabbed our attention as a young man stood beside a red Pontiac, shouting at the police officer to let him through.

In a flash, Detective Cornell was on his feet. "Stay here," he growled at me before rushing down the front steps, across the yard, and into the face of the fuming man.

"What's the problem here?" the detective demanded, towering above the young man by at least six inches.

The size of the detective didn't deter the man, however, as he puffed out his chest. "This is my girlfriend's house. I want to know what is going on?! Where is Lydia?"

"You're Eben Reitz?" the detective asked with as much shock in his voice as I felt. The young man looked as if he'd just graduated high school. James, Detective Cornell, and I ranked right up there with Mr. Padasky compared to Eben.

"Yeah, I'm Eben," the boy answered, pushing his dark hair away from his eyes. He reminded me a bit of Zac Efron in the movie *17 Again*.

Detective Cornell studied him for a moment. "I need you to come with me, Mr. Reitz," he finally said, motioning toward Lydia's front door that stood wide open. Then he looked over at me. "Kay, will you give Officer Vick your contact info so we can finish our conversation later?"

"Of course," I answered. Suddenly, a force pushed me toward the cement bannister of Mr. Padasky's porch, and I almost tumbled over it and into the now defunct rose bushes. James had bounded out of the house, jumped over the bannister, and was now rushing toward the Homicide Detective and Eben.

"You little punk!" James shouted as he drew menacingly closer to Eben. "What did you do to her?!"

Detective Cornell raised his hand and stepped between the two men. "Mr. McKellan, I need you to go back inside Mr. Padasky's house."

"I'm not going anywhere!" James roared.

I'd never seen him so angry. The James I knew was soft-spoken and polite. He never got ruffled over angry customers or complaints. Then again, it was his ex-wife who lay dead next door. Did he think Eben killed her?

"Mr. McKellan, I will not tell you again. If you don't return to Mr. Padasky's house and wait for me, I will take you downtown *with* me." By now, Detective Cornell had one hand on James' chest and the other on a rather calm Eben. Eben was watching James with an almost amusing grin on his face.

Smug punk.

"Come on, James!" Mr. Padasky said from behind me. "That boy ain't worth it."

Eben raised his chin in defiance towards Mr. Padasky, then shifted his blue eyes over to me.

"James, come inside," I pleaded. "I'll make you another cup of coffee. Or maybe some tea. Let Detective Cornell do his job."

When James took a step backward and turned in my direction, I caught Detective Cornell mouth the words *Thank You* to me.

Chapter 3

Smug Punks and Green Velvet

I stayed a bit longer with James and Mr. Padasky before heading home. James had refused to go back inside, but after some bribing with another cup of coffee - minus the alcohol - he agreed to sit on the front porch steps. I couldn't imagine what he must be feeling right now. I knew he hadn't liked Lydia toward the end of the relationship, but I was pretty confident that he'd still loved her deep down.

After I was confident that James would not confront Eben again, I retrieved my SUV from Lydia's driveway with permission from Officer Vick and drove home. Mr. Padasky's strong coffee lay in my stomach like a rotten battery, and since I had eaten nothing from breakfast on, I was starving.

When I walked into my house, I tossed my keys into the glass candy dish by the front door and made a beeline for the kitchen. The house wasn't large. The front door opened to a small living room with my bedroom to the right. Straight through the living room was the kitchen with another bedroom to the right of it. Past the kitchen was the laundry room and back door. The only bathroom was located to the left of this room. But what really made the property worth something was the large fenced-in backyard. It was basically three lots of empty land except for the heavy wooden swing and the cute she-shed I'd had installed on the back end of the property.

It was one of those Amish buildings that looked like a tiny house. I'd painted it white with gray trim, and inside the structure, the walls were painted a soft gray and outfitted with tearoom pink accessories and green velvet furniture; a small chaise and a reading chair. Drawers and bookshelves covered two walls with my collection from over the years. If I hadn't decided to work for my father, I would have been happily employed at a library or bookstore.

Owning a bookstore was a secret dream of mine. But the thought of breaking Dad's heart by not taking over Wellington's Pharmacy someday was too much to deal with right now. So, instead, I pushed those feelings of anxiety deep down to a simmer and preheated the oven for a frozen pizza. Tonight, I planned to take my pizza out to the shed and read until the fireflies came out, then sit on the tiny porch and watch them fly about before bed.

When the light went off on the oven, I popped the pizza in and ran to the bathroom for a quick shower. Although I'd scrubbed my hands of Lydia's blood at Mr. Padasky's house, I still felt nasty. I'd barely dried off and pulled on my yoga pants and a tank when my phone rang at the same time the oven went off. With one hand, I answered my cell and, with the other, opened the oven door with a pot holder and retrieved my dinner.

"Kay? Kay? Are you there?" My mom's voice came over my phone.

"Hey, Mom. Hold on. I'm taking a pizza out of the oven." I carefully placed the pizza pan on top of the glass surface. "Okay, it's out now."

"Oh, sweetie! I just heard that you found poor Lydia McKellan's body. Are you all right? Why didn't you call me?"

I shrugged, although Mom couldn't see me. "I'm fine, Mom. Everything happened so fast. Plus, when James arrived, I figured I should stay with him for a while."

"Yes. Poor man. How is he holding up?"

"One minute, he would cry over her; the next, he wanted to rip Lydia's boyfriend's head off."

"Oh my, does he think the boyfriend had something to do with it? Your father said Lydia was murdered. It's doubtful that it was random."

"I don't know. I mean, she did leave her back door unlocked most of the time, according to Mr. Padasky."

"Of course she did. We live in a small town that is relatively safe. We've only had a few murders, and those were by a truly deranged man. Remember those from a few years ago?"

I did remember. It was a serial killer, The Artist, but he had been caught and taken down in Charlotte by the well-known-about-town Detective Alec Graham. A dinging sound brought me out of my thoughts.

"Mom, I have to go. Someone is at my door."

"At seven o'clock in the evening? Don't hang up! Check and see who it is first. You can't be too careful."

I rolled my eyes. I highly doubted Lydia's murderer would want me, but despite scoffing at my mother's words, I picked up the heavy glass figurine my parents had given me last Christmas as I approached the door. Through the sheer curtain, I could make out a tall shadow.

As I peeked out the window, my heart stopped.

Chapter 4

Doe-Like Blue Eyes

My breath caught in my throat.

It took me a moment to gather my senses. "Mom, I have to go. Detective Cornell is here. I think he wants to finish talking with me about today."

"Detective Cornell? Who is he?"

"He's new on the force. I have to go." I disconnected the call, then hurriedly set the glass figurine down on the table by the door and straightened my tank. Did I have time to change clothes? Maybe a little black dress?

"Miss Wellington? Kay?" Detective Cornell's voice drifted through the door.

No time for a dress. He had seen me through the glass and knew I was standing on the other side of the door. I took a deep breath. I would just have to face the handsome detective wearing yoga pants instead of something pretty. At least I didn't have pizza sauce smeared down my shirt.

I opened the door to see the detective dressed in his suit pants and a dress shirt rolled up at the sleeves to his elbows, his tie askew.

"Hi. Are you all right?" I asked.

Detective Cornell grinned. "It's been a very hot, very long day, Miss Wellington."

"Kay," I remarked.

"Kay." The way he said my name made the hairs on the back of my neck rise. "I wanted to see if you were available to finish our conversation."

"Sure, come on in. I made a pizza. You're more than welcome to it."

Detective Cornell stepped inside. "Actually, I might take you up on that offer. I haven't eaten anything since a protein bar at breakfast." He ran his hand through his hair, and I noticed his sidearm for the first time. It must have been hidden by his suit jacket earlier today.

"Well, follow me." I led him into the kitchen, mentally checking the neatness of my house. Thank heavens, I kept it pretty organized and clean most of the time. "How were things between James and Eben after I left?"

Detective Cornell leaned against the refrigerator as he watched me retrieve two plates and slice the pizza with a cutter. "Not too bad. Lots of glaring. I take it the men had never met each other?"

I let out an immature snort before I could catch myself. Immediately, my cheeks heated. "No, they had never met. I'm sure James would have mentioned if Lydia had been dating a boy who looked like he missed his audition for *High School Musical*." I glanced at the detective, but I couldn't read his expression.

"I'll admit, I was a little shocked to meet Eben Reitz after seeing photos of Ms. McKellan and meeting her ex-husband."

I grabbed two bottles of water from the refrigerator and handed both to Detective Cornell. He followed me through the laundry room and out the back door as I carried the two plates piled high with pizza and a stack of napkins. "We'll eat outside. I have a little picnic table by the back porch."

Detective Cornell stopped short and surveyed the yard. "Wow. You own all this?"

"My grandparents left it to me. I've added a few things since, but yes, it's all mine."

After I set the plates on the wooden table, I continued, "I was shocked about Lydia and Eben too. After marrying James, why would she want to date someone so young? I mean, how old is he?"

Detective Cornell sat down on the bench. "He's of legal age, twenty-one. He just looks younger. The way you talk about James McKellan and the way I noticed you touching him on Mr. Padasky's front porch, I assume you two are a little more than friends?"

I narrowed my eyes at him from across the table. "Then you assume wrong, Detective Cornell."

"Pierce."

"What?"

"I'm technically off duty eating your pizza, so feel free to call me by my first name. It's Pierce."

I nodded. "Like Pierce Brosnan? Very cool of your parents." I smiled but then shook my head. "But as for James and I, you are so very wrong. I've known James since he was a pharmacy student working for my father during the summers. I attended his wedding to Lydia. He's my friend. And by touching him, I think you mean rubbing his arm to help calm him down after his confrontation with Eben."

Pierce took a bite of pizza while he thought about what I said. "So, you are not anything more with Mr. McKellan?"

"No, of course not. Why would you even ask that?"

"You two seem close."

"And because it might have given me a motive for murder?"

Pierce halted with his slice of pizza halfway to his mouth. "I didn't say that."

"You didn't have to say it. I watch a lot of murder mysteries and read even more cozies. So you think I may have felt some kind of competition with Lydia."

He dropped his pizza back onto the plate, the smile gone. "Did you?"

"No. I wasn't jealous of Lydia over anything. And I certainly wasn't competing for James' attention. As far as I know, Lydia wasn't after his romantic affections anymore."

"According to Mr. McKellan, Lydia was after his money. She was always calling him wanting more."

"Wanting more than what he already pays in alimony?"

"Apparently. Has he ever talked to you about it?"

I shook my head and pushed my glasses further up my nose. "No, James has never mentioned it to me directly. Please don't say anything, but my father let it slip one day that Lydia receives forty percent of James' income in alimony."

Pierce contemplatively took a bite of pizza as he slowly nodded his head. "Among other things," he said quietly.

"Like what?"

Pierce shrugged.

"How do you know this was a murder and that Lydia didn't just fall down the stairs and hit her head on the railing?" I asked.

"Is that what you think happened?"

"It could have," I offered. "Then she was so dizzy and senseless that she crawled into the family room."

"There would have been a blood trail. The only blood is on the post and in the family room. Is there anyone else you can think of who would want to hurt Ms. McKellan?"

"Hurt her, yes. Kill her, no. She was a demanding woman who tended to use people." I took a drink of water. What did I know about Lydia's personal life? "Have you questioned her sister?"

"Regan Tosta? Someone notified Miss Tosta of her sister's demise earlier today."

I swallowed the bite of pizza in my mouth and took another drink of water. "Rumor has it that Lydia co-owns Regan's little restaurant. She's more like a silent partner, though. I don't think I've ever known Lydia to work outside the home."

"Then what money was she living off of every month? How was she paying her bills?"

I shrugged. "I don't know. Maybe her sister paid her a percentage. On the other hand, maybe her support came from Eben."

At that, Pierce raised an eyebrow. We both knew Eben probably didn't make enough to support the likes of Lydia McKellan. "Eben Reitz is new to town, a college drop-out working at the Locklyn Market part-time. Staying most nights with Ms. McKellan."

"Where does he live when he isn't staying with her?" I asked.

"The owners of the grocery store also own an old storefront with an apartment on the second level next to the old junior high building. Eben rents from them."

I knew the place, the old Locklyn Junior High. During The Artist murders, a body had been found in the building, her ornate tattoo meticulously removed and framed beside her posed body. The crime had made national news. I shuddered.

"I remember the murder case at the old school a few years ago. It was how I learned that Detective Graham lives on my street."

Pierce's eyes grew wide. "Detective Graham lives here?"

"Well, down the street, in one of the brick houses. Sometimes I see him outside, mowing his lawn or grilling out with his fiancee."

Pierce took another long drink of water from his almost empty bottle. "I haven't met him yet. He left for vacation the same day I transferred in."

"I've talked with him at the pharmacy. He's nice. My family has known the mother of the girl he's marrying forever."

Pierce smiled as he pushed his paper plate away and leaned closer to me, his brown eyes studying mine. The scent of his subtle cologne wafted on the much-needed cooler breeze. "Actually, I would like to know more about you, Kay."

And just like that, the slice of pizza halfway to my mouth slid out of my hand and down my white tank. At the same time that I jumped up, embarrassed by my clumsiness and aggravated by the rare male attention, Pierce's phone rang.

He glanced at it and winced before handing me the stack of napkins I'd thankfully brought outside. "I have to take this."

"That's fine," I managed to say, still horrified as I blotted at the red stain, making it much, much worse. What started as a smear now looked like Buffy the Vampire Slayer had caught up with me.

"Cornell here," Pierce said, then listened intently as he stood and walked a few feet away. "Are you sure? I mean, it's just the preliminary lab work. If that's true, it changes everything." He listened again. "Okay, stay there. I'm on my way to the station."

When he hung up, he took a deep breath as he turned to face me, and I couldn't help but notice the rise and fall of his broad chest. *What was wrong with me?* I was acting as if I'd never seen a grown man before. Okay, admittedly, he was probably the first man I'd had in my backyard since I moved in five years ago. If you didn't count my dad. Or, the teenage boy who cut my grass every two weeks in the summer.

"Did you hear me, Kay?"

"Hmm?" No, clearly, I had not.

"I have to go, but I will need to stop in the pharmacy tomorrow. Are you working?"

"Yeah, I'll be there until five."

"What pharmacist will be on duty?"

"James. We're not like the big stores. Our pharmacists work five eight-hour days, not twelve hours."

He nodded. "Good. I'll see you tomorrow then." He leaned in, and for just a second, I thought Detective Pierce Cornell might kiss me. I studied his face, waiting for my cue. But instead, Pierce reached behind me and grabbed his bottle of water.

"See you in the morning, Kay."

I shut my slightly parted lips and forced my doe-like blue eyes back into their sockets. I needed to get it together. "See you in the morning, Pierce," I whispered to his back as he walked through the gate and headed to his car parked on the street.

As I gathered the plates and my water bottle, I started thinking about the phone call Pierce had received. What preliminary labwork changed everything? A tightening moved into my stomach, but it wasn't the pizza.

It was the sensation of dread.

Chapter 5

Together Together

"Well, look at you, all dressed up! Got a hot date tonight?" Miranda asked when I walked into the pharmacy at nine o'clock on the dot.

Nervously, I ran my hand down my blue and green floral A-line dress with the halter straps. "Why? Does it look bad?"

Miranda, dressed in our customary jeans, tee, and pharmacy smock, laughed as she looked me up and down. "No, girl! You look hot. But why are you wearing that dress today? And how are you going to stand in those heels back here?"

I glanced down at my black chunky heeled sandals with my freshly-painted bright pink toes peeping out. I couldn't very well say to Miranda that I wanted to look my utmost best because Detective Pierce Cornell had seen me at my worst *in my house* last night. So instead, I scrunched up my nose.

"I felt like something different today. That's all." I hung my purse in the back behind the shelving and retrieved my smock, checking to make sure I had a couple of pens in my pocket.

Miranda leaned against the pharmacy counter, watching me. "Have you seen James yet?"

"He's not here?"

"No, your dad unlocked the pharmacy gate and let me in. I texted James last night, you know, to check on him. He texted back that he needed some time alone."

"I'll ask Dad. Maybe James took the day off, and he's got a substitute coming in. I mean, I can hardly blame James for taking time to grieve." I started out from behind the counter when Miranda's voice stopped me.

"Why? Why would he grieve over that witch? She constantly used him, drained him dry, and we all know she was cheating on him while they were married."

"Miranda, that's enough," James said as he came around the corner. "Everyone can hear you."

Immediately, Miranda's face flushed. "There's no one in the store yet. It's just us."

James dropped his briefcase on the back counter, then turned to glare at Miranda. "My personal life is *my* personal life, Miranda. It's not up for discussion. Did you finish organizing this week's prescriptions?"

Miranda's eyes widened, and she looked like she was about to cry. "Not yet. I was going to do it after we received today's pharmacy order."

"Do it now," James growled as he jerked his white pharmacy jacket on before looking in my direction. I still hadn't moved from in front of the counter. I'd never heard James talk to any of us like that, especially Miranda, who was always running off at the mouth.

"Kay, are you off today?"

I shook my head. "No, I was headed into the back to ask Dad if *you* had taken the day off."

"Well, I didn't." James began punching the computer keys as he logged in. The tension in the store was palatable and I stole a glance at Miranda. She was slumped over on a stool in the corner filing the prescriptions from this week.

"James, I'm going to grab a cup of coffee. Do you want anything?" *Like a Prozac or a Valium?*

He was quiet for a moment, then looked up at me through the plexiglass and sighed loudly. "I guess a cup of coffee would be good."

I tried my best to smile. I couldn't imagine the stress and pain James must be feeling right now. "Miranda, you want anything?"

Miranda shook her head as she wiped a manicured hand over her cheek.

Great.

James, who was never hateful with anyone, had made our only other technician cry. I made my way into the back storeroom quietly, bypassing the break room, and straight into my father's office.

Dad looked up from his desk as I closed the door. "Good morning, Miss Katherine! Why, don't you look nice. Are you going somewhere?"

I ignored the question. Did I usually look gross? "Dad, have you talked to James?"

"Not yet. He was running late. I let Miranda in this morning. How is he?"

I sat down in the chair in front of the old wooden desk. "I think he is miserable. He's snapping at Miranda."

Thomas Wellington leaned forward, a frown creasing between his bushy white brows. "I've never heard that man snap at anyone," he said softly.

"He almost got into a fight with Lydia's boyfriend yesterday. Maybe it's not such a good idea that he be here right now."

"I messaged him last night and asked if he needed time off. He said no, Kay."

I pushed my bangs away from my face, silently scolding myself for fixing my hair and not wearing it in its usual ponytail. "I'm worried he won't be able to focus."

Dad nodded. "All right. Go back out there. I'll check in on him this afternoon."

I left the office and made two cups of coffee in the break room. But walking back to the pharmacy carrying two piping hot cups of coffee was a challenge while wearing my heeled sandals. So I slowed my pace to almost a crawl but paused completely when I rounded the corner and saw James holding Miranda. I could barely see the top of her redhead as James wrapped his arms tightly around her. One of his hands patted the back of her head gently.

I took a deep breath. It was too late to turn around and head back to the break room. I would spill everything for sure. "Could someone give me a hand?" I asked, pretending I had not witnessed something intimate between my coworkers.

James jumped away from Miranda and hurried over to the counter, retrieving one of the cups from my hand. "Thanks, Kay."

I kept my eyes locked on Miranda, who had turned away from me before resuming her duties with the files. Was James comforting her after hurting her feelings? Or was there something more between the two of them? Miranda did say she had texted James last night. How often did they talk after work?

My mind whirled the rest of the morning as I checked in and put away the daily delivery, talked with customers, and filled prescriptions. I also took note that neither James nor Miranda spoke much.

I was thankful for lunchtime. "I'm headed out for lunch. Anyone want anything?" I asked, removing my smock.

"I brought a protein shake," James said while on hold with a doctor's office on the phone.

"Miranda?"

Miranda shook her head. "I have a frozen dinner in the freezer."

"Just me, then? Okay," I said slowly. "I'll be back in a bit." Neither one answered.

I popped into the back and asked Dad if he wanted lunch. "Not today, sweetheart. I'm going home to have lunch with your mother," he said, his head down, focused on the spreadsheets in front of him.

Before leaving, I hesitated at the security video feed of the pharmacy. We had three cameras installed in the pharmacy. One facing the customer counter, one at the pharmacy counter behind the plexiglass, and one along the back of the pharmacy covering the controlled substances safe. Almost every square inch was covered with the camera angles. With the exception of the small kitchen alcove.

I peered a little closer at the monitor. Neither James nor Miranda were anywhere on the feed.

I hurried outside, watching the ground in front of me to keep from tripping over my sandals. Were James and Miranda together in the kitchen area? Were they *together* together? That was ridiculous. Maybe Miranda was in the kitchen warming up her dinner in the microwave, and James had run to the restroom. I shook my head. Our pharmacy didn't have public restrooms. James would have had to come back towards Dad's office to use one of the two restrooms. I would have seen him.

"Kay? Hi." A deep voice stopped me in my tracks beside my SUV.

"Detective! I mean, Pierce." I tucked a lock of hair behind my ear as I looked up at the sharply-dressed man standing before me, wearing that grin that made me melt like a schoolgirl.

Pierce's eyes scanned my outfit. "Wow. You look very pretty today."

"As opposed to yesterday evening when I was a bonafide mess."

His smile widened. "I didn't think you were a mess."

"My white tank looks better without pizza sauce," I answered. "I don't mean to be rude, but why are you here?"

"I need to speak to James." It was then that I noticed a uniformed police officer at the door to the store and a police car blocking the entrance. I must've been so caught up in my thoughts I hadn't heard the car pull in.

"What is this?" I asked.

Pierce frowned. "I need to speak with James...at the station." He turned and started for the door, but I ran after him.

"Why the station? I told you - everyone told you - James was here all day yesterday until he received the news about Lydia."

When he continued walking, I stepped in front of him, and he almost ran me over as I lost my balance in my sandals and started to fall backward. Pierce reached out and grabbed my arms with his strong hands. I held onto him even after he righted me in the parking lot. It had been a long time since a man had grabbed me like that. I'd forgotten how safe it made me feel.

"Um, Kay?"

I gazed up at Pierce, who looked uncomfortable as I held onto his arms. "Sorry, it's these shoes."

He smiled down at me. "If you'll excuse me, I have work to do."

I allowed him to pass but followed Pierce and the officer inside as they marched straight to the pharmacy counter.

"Mr. McKellan?"

James stood at the computer, the phone receiver up to his ear. "Detective Cornell. I'll be with you in a moment." Something passed over James' face. Was it worry? I glanced around the pharmacy. I couldn't see Miranda. Maybe she was in the restroom.

"Now, Mr. McKellan," Pierce said with a little more force.

James' eyes landed on me as he hung up the phone and came around the counter. "What is this about? I gave a statement yesterday."

Pierce took a deep breath and straightened, growing two inches taller. "We need you to come down to the station for questioning in the death of Lydia McKellan."

"What? I told you I was here until Kay called her father about finding Lydia's body." James' jaw clenched as he studied the detective.

"Preliminary lab work done on Ms. McKellan's prescription medication show that one of her bottles of generic Claritin was filled with ten-milligram tablets of generic Coumadin."

The look on my face had to match the expression on James' face. "What?" I whispered.

"According to bloodwork, your ex-wife had severe warfarin levels in her system, Mr. McKellan. The Medical Examiner estimates that she's been taking that high dosage for the last two months, perhaps longer."

James took a step back. "That's impossible. She had generic Claritin filled yesterday. It was loratadine. I swear, it was. I filled and counted it myself."

Pierce narrowed his eyes. "Yesterday's bottle was loratadine. But that's not what is in one of her old bottles. A bottle with your initials printed on the label. Do you know what happens to a healthy woman's body when she's given a high dosage of a blood thinner over a long period of time? A woman who imbibes in alcohol regularly?"

James' face paled. "Thinning of the blood, dizziness, nosebleeds, and severe internal bleeding," he whispered.

"Yes. Severe internal bleeding can lead to death. I need you to come with me to the station and explain how and why your ex-wife was given a blood thinner."

I followed Pierce, James, and the officer out of the pharmacy's front door, with my father asking Pierce what was happening. Miranda had come out from the backroom and now stood at the entrance to the store, visibly crying.

Although they were not handcuffing James, the officer did escort him into the backseat of the cruiser. But before the officer could shut the door, James touched the door handle. "Kay, I didn't do this. I would never intentionally give Lydia the wrong medication. Never."

"I know," I answered. "I'm going to find out who really killed Lydia."

Chapter 6

Kisses and Clues

"Kay? Where are you going?" Dad asked as I hurried to the truck.

"I'm going to need the rest of the day off. Maybe I can help James." I opened the SUV door and climbed inside just in time for a very tall, very ruggedly handsome detective to place his hand on my steering wheel.

"Whatever you are thinking, Kay, I need you to stop. Interfering in a police investigation is an offense." Pierce's brown eyes searched mine.

"I'm not interfering. I'm taking the day off to visit a friend."

He raised an eyebrow. "I literally heard you tell your father that you plan to help James."

"By visiting a friend." I smiled. Hopefully, he would let me go.

Pierce slowly backed away from my vehicle. "Despite what you heard inside about Ms. McKellan's medication, someone also violently slammed her head into the newel post on her stairs before shoving her into the family room. This we know from forensics. There may have been more than one person out to get her. I mean it, Kay. Let me do my job."

I nodded, then pulled out of the parking lot, my truck headed toward the Locklyn Market.

T he Locklyn Market was a smaller neighborhood store that hadn't been open very long. But, rumor had it, the owners, Mr. and Mrs. French, opened the store a couple of years ago because they were tired of shopping at our only grocery store in town, Food Park. They figured people would like the friendly atmosphere and small-town feel that the bigger-box store seemed to leave out.

They were right. The Locklyn Market was always busy.

I pulled into the parking lot in front of the plate glass store window and sat in the truck. What was I doing? How could I possibly find out who killed Lydia? If Pierce and the police were correct, then someone switched her medication, and then someone else - possibly - violently attacked her.

I watched the smaller brick building as customers entered and left through the automatic doors. I wasn't a detective. What made me think I could do anything? My phone rang, interrupting my thoughts, and I pressed the button on my steering wheel to answer.

"Hey, Dad."

"Kay, where are you?" Dad sounded both aggravated and resigned, if that was possible.

"I told you I needed the day off to visit a friend."

"Well, Miranda is a mess. She's crying all over the place, and no one has entered the store since James was taken away in the police car. Plus, I've already had two customers transfer all of their medication to another store."

"What are you saying?" I glanced at the clock, shocked by the display. I'd been wrestling with my thoughts and watching the doors to the Locklyn Market for the past forty-five minutes.

"Word is getting out that James may have given Lydia the wrong medication, which killed her. People might stop coming here."

"It's been less than an hour since they took James in for questioning, Dad. So we can't make that assumption yet."

A figure leaning against the brick building caught my attention as a pair of blue eyes watched me watching him.

"I've been in business a long time, Katherine. Word of mouth can make you or break you."

"Wellingtons are persistent. You taught me that. We'll get through this. Dad, I have to go." I disconnected the call, then turned off the engine. Eben Reitz gave me a half-smile as he turned and disappeared around the corner.

Like a final girl from some horror movie - or, more likely, one of the crazy girls who always ran towards trouble - I climbed out of the truck and smoothed my dress. It was now or never. I pressed the lock button on my keychain as I walked steadily toward the corner of the grocery store. The narrow paved alley contained a dumpster, but I couldn't see around it. I would have to walk the length of the alley.

Slowly, to watch my footing, I crept along the back wall of another brick building as I drew closer to the dumpster. Once around it, I sucked in my breath when my eyes met Eben's as he leaned against the wall next to the grocery store's metal back door.

"Hi," he said, taking his time, looking me up and down. He wasn't wearing the red apron that Locklyn Market employees wore. Instead, he was dressed in a pair of jeans and a tight white tee shirt.

"You're Eben."

He tilted his head. "You have me at a disadvantage. You know my name, but I don't know yours."

"It's Kay. I work with James, Lydia's ex-husband."

He nodded. "Yeah, I saw you with him yesterday. The detective said you found Lydia's body."

"I did."

"Well, why are you here now? I've watched you through the store window while you sat in your vehicle for the last hour. You're obviously here for a purpose."

"I, I want to ask you about...Lydia," I stammered out. His gaze had a way of pinning you where you stood.

"Go ahead. It's like I told the police, I don't have anything to hide," he said, his voice smooth as he tilted his head down again to peer at me through his lashes.

"How long have you and Lydia been together?"

"A few months."

"How did you meet?"

At this, Eben pushed himself away from the wall and slowly began crossing the alley toward me. "Is this really about Lydia? Or are you wanting to know more about me?" He stopped only two feet away.

I swallowed.

"Look," he continued, "I saw the way you were watching me yesterday. But right now, I'm dealing with the loss of my girlfriend. I'm not really looking for anyone new."

My mouth dropped open. "I'm not here to ask you out!"

Eben raised both his brows. "You're not?"

"No."

"Are you sure? Because you're dressed to impress today and hanging out in front of *my* workplace to talk to *me*." He pointed a finger at his chest.

"I'm here because the police are questioning James for Lydia's murder."

He took a few steps away from me. "So what? You think I killed her? I adored her. She was perfect. Perfect in every way."

"A neighbor said he heard the two of you fighting."

Eben suddenly moved closer to me again, so close that I pressed my back into the wall of the building next door. Eben placed his palm against the brick behind my shoulder, leaning toward my face, the slight scent of cinnamon coming from his breath.

"Mr. Padasky, I'm sure. That old man has it out for me. He had it out for Lydia too. Ask him about the property line and that ridiculous flower garden/shrine thing he has in his backyard."

"What-" I started, but the back door to the grocery store swung open, and Mr. French stood in the doorway.

"Eben, if you're done smooching with some girl, your break ended ten minutes ago."

Eben looked down at me and smiled. "Yeah, Mr. French, I'm done smooching with this girl."

I narrowed my eyes at him as he retreated into the building, but before I could explain to Mr. French what I was doing there, the man's eyes widened, and I heard him say to Eben before slamming the door, "Now you're dating Kay Wellington?"

Chapter 7

Revelations, DNA, and Watermelon (Maybe Not in that Order)

I picked up a chicken salad sandwich on sprouted bread and a bottle of water from a nearby restaurant and headed home. My mind shuffled to what Eben had told me about Mr. Padasky. What flower garden/shrine did the older man set up in his backyard? What would that have to do with Lydia? Maybe James knew.

I carried my food into the house and immediately kicked off my sandals. My feet were killing me. Barefoot was the only way to go. No sooner had I made my plate of food when a knock sounded at the door. Sighing loudly, I peeked through the glass to see the not-too-happy face of Detective Pierce Cornell.

Hesitantly, I opened the door.

Pierce raised his eyebrow at me again as he leaned against my door-frame. "So, where did you go today, Kay?"

I swallowed. News traveled too fast in this town. I opened the door wider. "Won't you come in? And shut the door behind you."

I walked back to the kitchen with the detective following me. He cleared his throat. "I stopped at the Locklyn Market a little bit ago to speak with Eben Reitz. Guess what the owner Ralph French had to say when I interviewed him about his employee's character?"

I shrugged as I added a few pretzels to my plate and offered the bag to Pierce. He shook his head.

"He said Eben is a player. As a matter of fact, he was seen kissing a girl only minutes before I showed up."

When I didn't answer but stood dumbfounded in my kitchen, Pierce placed both hands on my kitchen table and leaned forward, his eyes searching my soul. "Why didn't you tell me you are involved with Eben?"

"Because I'm not."

"He was the friend you drove off to visit today."

"No. I mean, yes, but he's not a friend. I wanted to ask Eben more questions to understand what really happened to Lydia."

He narrowed his eyes. "Why were you seen kissing him?"

I rolled my eyes as I sighed. "I didn't kiss him. Mr. French opened the door to see Eben leaning over me, and he made an assumption." I laughed. "There were no kisses. Do I look like the type of girl who would kiss a guy to get info out of him?"

Pierce's gaze traveled down my dress, and I swallowed hard. When his gaze met mine again, I managed to ask, "What happened with James at the station?"

Pierce straightened. "I can't share that information with you."

I slid my plate across the table to him. "Even for half a sandwich from the best deli in town? Homemade chicken salad. And I can throw in some sliced seedless watermelon," I answered in a sing-song voice.

Pierce peered down at the plate, then back to me. "Okay, only if you add in a bottle of water. But you're not going to like it. James still had a physical relationship going on with his ex-wife."

Chapter 8
Blood and Tulips

I almost dropped the container of watermelon I was carrying from the refrigerator to the sink. I was thankful my back was to Pierce.

"Did you hear me, Kay? James had resumed a physical relationship with his ex-wife."

I poured several pieces of sliced watermelon into a bowl before turning to face Pierce's scrutiny. "He told you this?"

"Yes. He claims she came to him and wanted to resume their relationship."

I set the bowl down with a thud on the table. "Doesn't make any sense. James couldn't stand Lydia. Everyone knew it."

Pierce popped a piece of watermelon into his mouth and chewed, lost in thought. Finally, he asked, "What better way to keep it under wraps? Make everyone believe he hated Lydia while secretly having an affair with her. Not to mention, a way to somehow jab at her new boyfriend."

I shook my head as I sat down at the table and motioned for Pierce to join me. "That doesn't sound like James. He doesn't seem like the type of man to volunteer to share a woman. He knew Lydia had a boyfriend who spent nights in her house. While they were married, he was crazy about her. It broke his heart when she turned on him."

Pierce shrugged. He must have been hungry as he'd inhaled half of the sandwich.

I frowned. "Why did James tell you this? What led up to it?"

"Forensics found traces of James' DNA on Lydia."

"Not Eben's?" I asked, shocked by the news. My lunch was looking less appealing by the minute.

Pierce stopped eating to look me straight in the eye, that forceful detective personality peeking from behind his eyes. "I didn't say we didn't find Eben's DNA too."

I almost gagged. "I think I'm going to be sick. So what are you saying?"

He took a deep breath and leaned back in the old wooden kitchen chair. "Lydia visited James the night before her death, then went home to Eben."

"Is that why she and Eben were heard arguing that night? Because of James?"

"I don't know yet. I'm going back to speak with Eben later this evening." He took a drink of water. "I shouldn't be telling you any of this."

"Why are you?" I asked before taking a bite of a pretzel.

"I've already dismissed you from the list of suspects, and you are the first person in this little town that seems nice and normal. You seem like the type who knows how to keep a secret. According to your neighbors, you're known as a "good girl" who everyone can rely on. Honest, trustworthy, sweet. Nothing like George Padasky."

I laughed. "To be fair, people like Mr. Padasky are rare in Locklyn."

Pierce smiled with a grin that lit up his chocolate-brown eyes. "That's good to know."

I pushed my plate away to lean forward on my elbows. *Was I really this bold?* "Tell me about yourself. Why did you transfer to Locklyn? What made you want to work in the homicide division?"

Something danced in Pierce's eyes that I couldn't quite identify. "I wanted a change from big city crime. I'd heard great things about Locklyn and the police force here. But to be honest, I feel like a fish out of water. I don't know anyone, and there seems to be a lot of small-town politics in play. I've been a cop for ten years, but the guys on the force treat me like a rookie."

"I'm sure they will accept you soon. Is that why you were so demanding when you came for James this afternoon?"

"What do you mean *demanding*? Because I asserted my authority? That's who I am, Kay. Lead Homicide Detective on this case." He finished the watermelon on his plate and took another long drink of water.

"It was just a different guy than the Pierce Cornell sitting across from me right now." I studied his face as he seemed to be lost in thought again. Where did he go when his eyes glazed over like that?

"Well," he managed after a long pause. "That guy gets answers. *This* guy enjoys the company of beautiful and clever women at lunchtime."

My cheeks heated, but I refused to drop my gaze. "You share lunch with a lot of beautiful and smart women?"

With that, Pierce leaned forward, his face only inches from mine. "Just you," he breathed. As if on some terrible cue from the lets-not-let-Kay-have-any-romance-in-her-life powers that be, my cell phone rang.

I tore my eyes from Pierce's to see Wellington's Pharmacy pop on the screen. "Sorry, I have to take this," I mumbled as I stood, then walked into the laundry room. Not that Pierce couldn't hear the conversation - barely a wall separated the kitchen from the laundry area.

"Dad? Now isn't a good time."

"Katherine, I need you to come in. Miranda left early." Dad sounded exhausted. It had been a while since he had had to operate both the front of the store and the pharmacy, although he was a pharmacist and could easily handle the orders. But apparently, he was doing the job of three people.

I sighed.

"Okay, I'm on my way."

After disconnecting the call, I returned to find Pierce at the front door. "I should be getting back too. I plan to talk with Eben some more, as well as James. Thanks for lunch."

I drew nearer to him as he spoke until I was close enough to pick up the subtle scent of mint gum. "Thanks for stopping by. I'm glad I could clear up your misconception of my relationship with Eben."

Pierce winced. "When Mr. French told me he saw you, I'll admit I was stunned. Of course, now that I know the truth, I'm not nearly as alarmed. But you know what would make me feel even better?" he asked innocently enough, but his eyes lit up playfully.

I could think of all kinds of things. Probably not what he was thinking, though.

Pierce continued, "I would feel better if you left the investigation to me. You do not want your name associated with a murder investigation. Trust me on this."

I crossed my heart with my index finger. "I promise. I'll stay out of it. But, if I hear anything, I'll call the station."

Pierce watched my finger trace over my heart and ever-so-lightly bit his lower lip, sending a shiver through me. He reached into his suit jacket pocket and produced a business card.

"Here. Don't bother with the station. You can call me directly."

My heart gave a little flutter as I took the card and nodded. After Pierce left and I shut the door, I may have done my version of a celebratory dance for a full five minutes before sliding my sandals on again and heading out to the pharmacy.

T he store was utterly dead when I arrived. Not even a crow hung around the roof to squawk at me like they usually did. This was strange. It was only three o'clock, and the store was open for another two hours. We were the second pharmacy in Locklyn - the other inside of the Food Park - and typically, customers came in bursts, but this seemed odd.

"Thank heavens you're here," Dad said when I walked in, then groaned when he saw me look around the empty store. "I told you. No one wants to shop here now."

"Nonsense, Dad. It's beautiful outside. I'm sure people are just outside enjoying the day."

Thomas Wellington did not look convinced. "We will see, I suppose. James called. He'll be on duty tomorrow."

"They let him leave?"

"What can they hold him for? He was nowhere near Lydia when she died. I don't know how they will prove that James filled last month's Claritin script with Coumadin." He moved off the stool and headed towards the front counter. "I've checked our inventory of both drugs. It's up-to-date. I'll be right back."

"Dad, why did Miranda leave?" I asked, stopping Dad in his tracks in front of the double doors that led to the back rooms.

"She was a mess, Kay. I've never seen her like that. She was sobbing and saying that James didn't deserve this. That this was all Lydia's fault." He shrugged. "She wasn't making a bit of sense."

I glanced at the clock. We closed at five. Would I really be breaking a promise if I drove to Miranda's apartment? As a friend and co-worker, I was concerned about her. Plus, I wanted to find out what this morning was about when I'd seen James holding her.

My gaze landed on Pierce's business card sticking out of my purse. There was no need to bring Pierce into this if it was nothing. It probably was nothing. It's not like Miranda would do something to Lydia to have James to herself. A sinking sensation hit my stomach for the third time today. People did crazy things for love.

Crazy enough to murder someone's ex-wife?

Then there was Mr. Padasky's backyard. Eben said the older man was territorial over the property line and a specific area. That tidbit of info wasn't worth mentioning to Pierce either. I could simply ask James about it.

But part of me secretly wanted a reason to call Pierce Cornell.

I finished my shift and helped Dad count the money and lock up for the evening. After setting the alarm, I climbed into my Trailblazer. What to do first? Drive to Miranda's and ask her about her relationship with James, or hunt down James and ask him about Mr. Padasky's backyard and *his* relationship with Lydia?

I decided to question Miranda first. Part of me was very much disgusted with James if he had resumed a physical relationship with Lydia. Why would he do that? Was he desperate?

The drive to Miranda's was short and uneventful. The redheaded pixie lived in an apartment building near Food Park. I parked next to her beat-up little Nissan and made my way to a white door surrounded by brick. It took me knocking three times before a weepy-eyed Miranda opened the door.

"Hey," I said, taking in her fleece buffalo plaid pajama bottoms and black tank top. "Dad said you left early, and I wanted to check on you. May I come in?"

Miranda hesitated, then moved away from the door. "Sure."

Fast food wrappers and mail on every square-inch surface cluttered the small living room. . Dirty clothes littered the floor in front of the couch.

"Sorry for the mess, Kay. I wasn't expecting anyone."

"Mess? No, you should see my place," I answered and laughed, trying to take away any embarrassment Miranda might feel. I moved a pile of clothes from one end of the couch and sat down. "Is everything okay, Miranda?"

Miranda walked into the attached kitchen and grabbed two cans of Dr. Pepper. She handed me one. "How can anything be okay? James was arrested for Lydia's murder."

"He wasn't arrested. Pierce, I mean, Detective Cornell, just wanted to question him about the possible pharmacy mistake. Dad told me that James called and will return to work tomorrow."

"Really?" She raised her head, hope written across her face.

"Yes, I'm sure the police will find Lydia's true killer and find that whatever happened to her medicine bottle was a mistake. But, honestly, I'm not sure how a mix-up like that would have occurred."

"Coumadin and Claritin both start with C. We organize the generics by their brand names. Their generics would have been near each other on the shelves."

I blinked. "Miranda, the generic Claritin is an over-the-counter drug. We keep it with the other fast-mover drugs near the pharmacy counter. It's nowhere near the warfarin. You know that."

Miranda frowned, and I made a mental note to check the inventory. Dad had said he checked the stock of both drugs, and they were correct, but Miranda appeared confused. Dread landed in my belly.

"Miranda, I need to ask you something."

She sat down opposite me in a chair on top of another pile of clothing. "What is it?" she asked, taking a sip of her drink.

"What's going on between you and James?"

Miranda almost choked on her mouthful of Dr. Pepper. "What? What do you mean?" she stammered out.

"I came around the corner this morning and saw James hugging you. What was that about?"

"You didn't tell anyone, did you?" Miranda asked, her eyes wide.

I shook my head.

I watched as Miranda stood and began pacing back and forth in the living room. "I was upset over Lydia, that's all. Then when James snapped at me, it was like a floodgate opened. I don't know why I'm so emotional."

I could feel the space between my brows begin to furrow. If I kept this up, I would have to invest in Botox soon.

"It looked like there was more to it than that."

Miranda froze mid-step. "More?"

"I'm no romance expert, but it seemed more intimate than that."

Miranda narrowed her eyes. "You're right. You're no romance expert."

Ouch.

She continued, "You don't know anything about my friendship with James. He's a really cool guy. He always listens to me and gives me advice when I need it." She placed both hands on her hips.

"Perhaps I misunderstood," I contended. "I always thought you liked James. Maybe wanted something more from him?"

Miranda narrowed her eyes even more, making them appear as tiny slits, and I wondered how much longer I should push this subject. "It's not like that between us."

"Because you don't want something more? Or he doesn't?"

Miranda raised her chin in defiance. "I think you should go home now, Kay. I'm tired."

I stood and thanked Miranda for the can of soda pop but stopped as she opened the front door. "Miranda, did you know that James and Lydia had an ongoing sexual relationship?"

Miranda paled.

"I'm going to take that as a no," I said slowly.

Miranda leaned heavily on the door. "I wondered if they were," she whispered. "I called him the other night, and I could hear Lydia in the background."

"The other night? The night before she came into the pharmacy? The night before she died?"

Miranda nodded. "I could hear Lydia cooing something to James. He was at home. He grumbled something back to her, then told me he had to go."

"Do you know why he would go back to Lydia? Why would he take her back while she was with Eben?"

Miranda shrugged. "I don't know. She was evil personified. James needs a good woman." She lowered her voice until it was barely audible. "I could've been that woman. I would have made him happy."

Two hours later, I found myself huddled in Lydia's backyard, wearing a pair of short denim shorts, a pink front-knot tee shirt, and a fuchsia ball cap pulled down over my eyes; not exactly the covert-mission outfit one would expect. But it was too hot to wear black leggings and a turtleneck to skulk around.

The neighborhood was quiet for a Tuesday evening. I hadn't seen hide nor hair from Mr. Padasky next door. Since Lydia's house was marked as a crime scene, Eben must be sleeping at his apartment now. I crouched closer to the fence line to peer over into Mr. Padasky's backyard. I could see several flowerbeds made from brick winding through the yard, but I couldn't make out anything else.

Maybe if I slipped into the very back of his property on the other side of his shed, I could see the yard a little better. I maneuvered my white canvas shoes around the stacked cinder blocks separating Lydia's fence from Mr. Padasky's wooden shed. I barely squeezed through. From this vantage point, Mr. Padasky shouldn't be able to see me if he happened to glance out one of the windows facing the backyard.

The extensive flower gardens made an "S" shape through the yard. Specific flowers were planted in six-foot sections. He had sections of different colored roses, irises, marigolds, petunias, and several that I had no idea what they were called. In the midst of these, sat the ugliest gnomes ever created by man. This had been his wife's gardens. He'd let the other flower beds go in the front yard, but was still maintaining these.

The shed set catty corner along the fence line with the wooden door facing the opposite corner of the property. I pressed my body against the door of the shed. What was it about the yard that would have Mr. Padasky riling up at Lydia and Eben? The property line seemed to be separated by a wooden privacy fence for most of the length and then a tall chain-link fence that reached the alley. From what I could tell, the yards looked uniform.

This was a bust. There was nothing in the backyard to indicate why Mr. Padasky had problems with Lydia, other than the two of them had strong personalities.

Suddenly, voices cut through my thoughts. It sounded like Mr. Padasky and another man was in the house. The voices came closer.

I tried the wooden shed door, and it easily opened. I slipped inside and closed the door. I could barely make out anything in the darkness, with only slits between the slats allowing the evening light to make its way inside. The voices got louder, and I realized the two men were walking through the backyard.

Crap.

I would have to wait it out until they left before I could escape. I crouched near the floor and swallowed the urge to sneeze in the musty building. As my fingers brushed the floorboards, a strong metallic scent reached my nostrils. I maneuvered myself until I could silently reach into my back pocket and withdraw my cell phone. I flipped on the flashlight app and shined it over the floor.

Not two feet from me lay a long, yellow wooden handle attached to a red metal shovel head. I peered a little closer, then let out a gasp. The red on the metal shovel head wasn't painted.

It was blood.

Chapter 9

The Search

B^{*lood.*}

B *lood.*

The realization hit me with such force that I launched away and fell backward, pushing the shed door open and falling out onto the well-manicured lawn, slamming my head on the grass. I blinked several times, taking in the evening sky's pink, orange, and red hues. That is, until a grumpy-looking Mr. Padasky and a surprised yet aggravated Detective Pierce Cornell stared down at me.

"Katherine Wellington! What on earth are you doing in my shed?" Mr. Padasky yelled down at me as if I'd lost my hearing when I hit the back of my head.

I didn't answer right away. Not just because I was slightly dazed but because I had no idea what to say. *Hey, I was snooping in your yard to see if maybe you killed Lydia over your flower garden. By the way, I found a bloody shovel in your shed.*

No. None of that would work.

Except I didn't need to say anything. Pierce looked from my face to the open shed door, then left my side when something caught his attention. Mr. Padasky helped me to a sitting position.

"Mr. Padasky, what is this?" Pierce held the handle of the shovel up for us to see.

Mr. Padasky frowned. "It's a shovel, Detective. They don't have shovels wherever you come from?" The elderly man steadied himself as my legs finally gathered enough strength to hold me upright.

"Don't be smart, Mr. Padasky. Is this blood on the shovel?" Pierce held the shovel higher as he inspected the metal head.

The man stepped a little closer to it. "I reckon it is. I killed a raccoon with it the other day."

Pierce studied him. "You're telling me you killed a raccoon with this shovel? That this blood is from an animal?"

"That's what I'm saying, all right." Mr. Padasky huffed out the words as if Pierce was somehow offending him.

"Well, I will need to take this to the station and have it tested. Are you aware that the back of Lydia McKellan's head received trauma from an impact before she died?"

Mr. Padasky's jaw clenched. "I'm aware, but I didn't bash the woman's head in if that's what you're implying. I wouldn't ruin a good shovel by dousing it with her blood."

Pierce opened his mouth and then shut it again quickly. I shrugged when he looked at me. It was Mr. Padasky. What could you expect from the older man? He'd hated Lydia.

When Mr. Padasky turned to saunter back into his home, Pierce focused on me. "Exactly why were you hiding in the shed?"

I sighed. "It was something Eben said to me."

When I didn't continue, Pierce prompted, "And?"

"Can we leave the yard? I don't want Mr. Padasky to hear me," I whispered.

Pierce nodded, and I followed him out the backyard gate to his unmarked silver police car. I watched as he deftly removed a plastic evidence bag from the trunk and slid it over the shovel, securing it with sticky tape before placing it in the trunk and slamming the door.

"Well?"

I pressed my lips together. "I thought Lydia's head hit the newel post, and that's what killed her?"

"Answer the question, Kay."

He was not going to like this. "Eben told me Mr. Padasky had it out for Lydia and him. Something about a flower garden-shrine-thing and the property line. I wanted a closer look without alarming anyone, so I snuck into his backyard but didn't see anything."

"Why were you in the shed?"

"I heard voices and ducked inside. I planned to leave when the backyard was clear again."

Pierce studied me for so long that I finally dropped my gaze to my shoes. Until he took a step closer, and I could feel the heat from his body through his clothes. Slowly, he lifted my chin with two fingers until I stared into his brown eyes.

"You promised me you would stop this amateur sleuthing."

I exhaled a breath that I was unaware I'd been holding inside. "I didn't think it was worth mentioning yet. Of course, when I found the bloody shovel, you were the first person I planned to call."

Pierce dropped his hand from my face, and I instantly missed the touch. "That is until you fell out of the shed. What if that hadn't been me standing there? What if whoever attacked Lydia had been standing there instead?"

I didn't answer. I didn't want to think about what might have happened. "Do you believe Mr. Padasky's story? I mean, I can see him bashing a poor defenseless animal's head in, but not Lydia's."

Pierce moved around me towards his driver's side door. "I guess we will wait until the lab gets back to me and go from there. Where's your car?"

"Two doors down. Why were you here talking to Mr. Padasky?" I asked, following him around the car.

Pierce let out an exasperated sigh. "He reported that someone had dug into one of his flower beds, uprooting all the flowers as if they were searching for something. Since he lives next door to the crime scene, I wanted to check it out."

"Nothing looked disturbed to me."

"It was the flower bed closest to the back door near the steps."

I nodded. I hadn't paid much attention to anything up against the house. My focus had been on the gardens winding through the lawn.

"Well, it doesn't appear Mr. Padasky plans to press trespassing charges on you, but I suggest you go home and stop interfering." His gaze pinned me to the sidewalk as he took in my outfit. "You're not the blend-in-to-the-environment type."

I crossed my ankles, keenly aware that his gaze traveled back up to my face. My cheeks heated when he reached my eyes.

"Will you at least tell me what you learn about the shovel?"

"Kay," he sighed loudly.

"Please?"

His mouth twisted as he considered my words. "All right, but you can't breathe a word of it to anyone."

I smiled. "Of course not, Detective. What do you think someone was searching for in Mr. Padasky's flower bed?"

Pierce glanced up at the house over my shoulder. "I don't know. He denies having anything buried out there. You know what? I'm starving." His eyes met mine again as a playful smile broke out on his face. "Want to have dinner with me? My treat this time. I owe you two meals."

My heart leaped out of my chest, and I mentally willed it back into place. "Yeah, I would like that. Just let me go home and change into something nicer and take an ibuprofen."

"Oh, that's right. You hit your head pretty hard." He reached up and cradled the back of my head in his huge hand. I held my breath. "Would you rather have dinner tomorrow night? So you can rest?"

I shook my head. "No, I'm fine. Really. Plus, I'm sure I'm not supposed to go to sleep for a while after a bang to the head."

Pierce suddenly pulled me closer to him, his gaze serious. "You're right. You shouldn't sleep alone tonight."

My eyes widened.

Pierce blinked. "I mean, you shouldn't be left alone for a while."

A sudden siren blip made Pierce and I jump. Pierce dropped his hand from the back of my head.

"Detective Cornell, here you are," Police Chief Sanders spoke to Pierce, but his eyes landed on me.

"Yes, sir," Pierce answered.

"Hello, Chief," I said, smiling ear-to-ear. I'd known Chief Sanders for as long as I could remember.

"Kay," he answered, his car idling in the street. "Cornell, I need to speak with you privately."

Pierce jumped again as he made his way to the cruiser. I took this as my cue. "Good night, gentlemen!" I waved.

Pierce looked back at me and smiled as he motioned with his cell phone. He would call me later.

Chief Sanders did not look thrilled at all.

Chapter 10

Little Treasures

I floated all the way home in my car. Thank Heavens, I only lived a short drive from Mr. Padasky's house. I rushed inside and jumped into the shower. I had a sort-of date with Pierce. But as the hot water stung the back of my head where I had slammed it into the ground, my mind wandered back to Mr. Padasky's shed. Had the older man really killed a raccoon with that shovel?

Or had he used it on Lydia?

I would have never thought the frail, old man was physically capable of swinging that shovel hard enough to hurt anything. But, then again, Mr. Padasky had served as a young man in the military. He'd told me once that that was how he'd contracted Hep C - from the needles he and his buddies shared for their tattoos.

But why would he want to kill Lydia? Surely some property dispute wasn't worth killing her over. Mr. Padasky complained about the loud noise and parties Lydia and Eben threw, but would the man knock her head into the newel post?

Maybe Mr. Padasky was telling the truth. But, if that was the case, why did Eben bring up the property line? To throw suspicion off himself?

I shook my head as I turned the water off. This was exactly why I hadn't become a cop. I should leave it to Pierce and the Chief.

After I dressed in a blue halter dress and reapplied my makeup, I picked up my cell phone. There was a text from Pierce. But, unfortunately, it wasn't him declaring his undying love for me.

Pierce: **Hey, Kay. I'm sorry about this, but the Chief wants me to stay at the station longer. More paperwork. I'm sorry. Raincheck?**

I sighed. It had been too good to be true.

Me: **That's no problem. We can reschedule.**

I started to toss my phone over to the couch in frustration when the thought occurred to me. I was already dressed. It wasn't late out. I could take advantage of my free time. Maybe now was a good time as any to drop in on James.

James' apartment was located in a much swankier area than Miranda's little place. These looked more like all-brick townhouses. I stood on the concrete porch and took a deep breath before ringing the doorbell. I'd tried hard to think of ways to broach the subject of James' relationship with Lydia without sounding like a weirdo.

Nothing had come to me yet.

I pushed the doorbell and suddenly heard music playing inside. After a minute, the door opened, and James stood there looking surprised.

"Kay! What are you doing here?"

I forced a smile. "I wanted to check in on you. I heard the police sent you home. Are you okay?"

James' eyes flitted briefly, and I wasn't sure what that was about. Was he hiding something? "Sure. I'm fine. Come on in."

He moved away from the door, and I entered a rather large living room with white walls, gray carpet, and a soft leather gray sectional. The far end of the room housed a white stone fireplace. James motioned for me to sit on the sectional as he sat on a nearby matching recliner.

"Well, this is nice! I don't think I've ever been here," I said, noting that the room lacked personal items like photos and books. James had been living here for about a year. Why wouldn't he have given the place a lived-in look by now? "Is this the formal living room?"

"The *formal* living room?" James laughed. "Kay, what you see is what you get. This is the living room, and there is a small dining room and kitchen through that doorway." He pointed at the doorway above my shoulder.

"Well, it is very nice. How are you holding up?"

James took a deep breath as he relaxed against the chair. "I wish Lydia was still alive. She drove me insane, and I didn't understand the things she did, but...she was Lydia." He shrugged and looked away.

I swallowed. "So, you and she were still close?"

His gaze darted back to mine. "What do you mean?"

"I mean, you still loved her." The heat moved into my cheeks, and I could feel the slightest trickle of sweat making its way down the back of my dress, but I refused to drop my gaze.

James was quiet for a moment. "Yeah, I guess I did still love her." He stood and walked to a minibar beside the fireplace. "Can I get you anything?"

"No, thank you."

He poured himself a drink from a tall decanter and then settled back into his chair. "For everything that Lydia did, there was something about her. She was charismatic. She was beautiful. When she wasn't demanding, she had a way of turning her eyes on me that made me feel like I was the only man in the universe. As if her world revolved around me." He took a huge gulp of his drink. "But when she was demanding, when her attention wavered, she was unbearable. Almost evil."

I silently agreed with James. Not about the whole "Her world revolved around me" thing, but the evil part.

I took another deep breath. It was now or never. "Were you still seeing her?"

James narrowed his eyes. "Seeing her?"

I dropped my gaze. I was no detective. Would he know that Pierce had divulged information to me about his relationship with Lydia because of my line of questioning? "I mean, the way you talk about her. It sounds like maybe you still had a physical attraction toward Lydia."

James leaned forward in his chair, his brown eyes searching mine. "Kay, what is this really about?"

"You asked for my help. I'm trying to get to the bottom of what happened to Lydia so that the police will stop looking at you as a suspect. I would be grateful if you could tell me the truth. The truth about your relationship with Lydia. I want to help you." The last sentence came out more like a whiny plea, and I almost kicked myself.

He leaned back into the recliner. "I know I asked for your help. It's not fair that I keep things from you." He stared at the rim of his glass. "Sometimes Lydia would come around. Sometimes she would want to...spend time with me."

"Spend time with you," I repeated the words slowly. Any faster, and my digestive tract would probably spew today's lunch.

"You know what I mean," he answered quickly. "At first, I thought, why not? I knew she was with Eben, but I didn't know him. Plus, it almost felt like I was getting something back for all the money I sink into her every month. Do you know I pay for her health insurance? Still? I pay the mortgage on that house. I even make the car payments for her."

"James, did you tell the police all this?"

He nodded. "Yes. And I know it gives me motive."

I decided to change the subject. "Was there a property line dispute with Mr. Padasky?"

James' brows knitted in confusion. "Property line dispute? No. The lines are well marked. I never had any problems with Mr. Padasky."

"But Lydia did?"

James gave a soft laugh. "Lydia and Mr. Padasky never liked each other. Everything she did aggravated him. His mere existence was an offense to Lydia. I never understood why she chose to live in the house after the divorce."

"Someone said that Mr. Padasky has a flower garden or shrine built for his wife in the backyard and that he is overprotective about it."

James shrugged. "I don't know. Mrs. Padasky had beautiful flower gardens. In the last years of her life, when the dementia got bad, she'd started hiding things out there. One time, I was working on the pool when she hollered for me. She asked me if I'd seen where she had buried her silver comb. I asked her why she would bury her comb. She said it was because she didn't want anyone to steal her treasures, and her comb was made of real silver. She told me she'd buried all her treasures. Maybe Mr. Padasky believes she hid more things in the flower gardens."

"But do you think she really buried expensive items out there? Or just things she felt were important to her?"

"At her funeral, Mr. Padasky told me he was missing quite a few things from the house. He described them as *nice* things. I don't know if he meant expensive or not. He said he didn't know where his wife had hidden them as the disease progressed quickly."

I considered his words. Maybe someone else knew about Mrs. Padasky's "treasures" and decided to dig them up for themselves. Maybe Lydia had seen someone.

Maybe she'd seen too much.

Chapter 11

White Caterpillars

The next morning was glorious. Mostly because I was off work. Miranda was working the entire day, and James was on duty. After tugging on a pair of cut-off shorts and a vintage '80s tee, I pulled my hair up into a bun. Are the 1980s really vintage now? Although James swore I had been working for my father as a tech for 15 years, it was closer to 12 years in the pharmacy. But I had grown up working in the store unpacking the gift items and blowing up balloons for customers. It was when I turned 18 that I finally asked if I could work as a pharmacy technician-in-training. Not too long after that, I passed my national certification.

I still wanted to run a bookstore, though. Maybe I could talk Dad into expanding one corner of the store. Maybe rename it Wellington's Pharmacy *and Books*. There was a thought.

Slipping my feet into flip-flops, I made my way to my car.

Last night, I made the decision to visit Mr. Padasky first thing today. I wanted to understand what "little treasures" his wife may have buried in the flower gardens. And why someone might have been willing to kill for them.

Okay, so it was a long shot. But, even if Mrs. Padasky had buried some silver items in the flower beds, would someone murder Lydia if she had seen them? Kill her over something like that? Part of me said no.

But I still felt like I should check it out. Plus, I didn't believe that Mr. Padasky was the one who killed Lydia. *Sure*, he hated her. *Yes*, he knew the back door was unlocked. *Okay*, he knew Eben wasn't home. *And* he left the pharmacy before Lydia did. Then there was the bloody shovel.

Hmm.

All these thoughts were swirling through my head when I parked my Trailblazer in front of Mr. Padasky's house.

Don't back out now, Kay, I told myself. *James needs you to clear his name. Pierce and the rest of the police force are still looking at him as a suspect. You can do this!*

A knock on my car window made me yelp like a terrified poodle. Mr. Padasky stood staring at me through the glass, a frown pulling his caterpillar brows together. I pressed the button and lowered the window separating us.

"Kay? What are you doin' round here again?"

"Um, hi, Mr. Padasky. I was hoping I could speak to you. About your wife."

The man made a hrmph sound, then stepped back from the vehicle. "Well, come on in then. Early mornings is the only time I can work on the yard because of the heat. I guess it can wait another day," he grumbled.

I hurriedly rolled the window up, shut off the engine, and then joined him on the front porch of his home. I glanced around the front yard. The grass was neatly trimmed, but he'd allowed the flowers to die. Unlike the flower gardens in the backyard, these flower beds were in a sad state of decay.

As I followed him inside, I asked, "What exactly are you doing in the front yard?"

He half-turned. "What?"

"You said you were out to do yard work before it got too hot outside. Are you planning on redoing the flower beds in the front yard?"

Mr. Padasky frowned and motioned for me to sit. "No, not right now. I was gonna weed-eat the edges of the lawn."

"Oh." *Great answer, Kay. Now make sure to stare at the man, stupified. Good job!*

"Kay, can I get you somethin' to drink? How about some iced tea?"

"I would love that. Thank you."

I watched as the man slowly shuffled into the kitchen. I needed better questions. Pronto. I glanced around the living room. I couldn't see anything of real value displayed throughout the house. Just some knick-knacks and glass vases. These were items I could pick up from the local dollar store. Maybe Mrs. Padasky hadn't had anything of monetary value to hide.

Mr. Padasky returned and handed me a tall glass of iced tea. "Thanks."

I waited until he lowered himself into the chair across from me. "Mr. Padasky, I'm sorry about yesterday. Me being in your shed. I didn't want to bother you, but someone mentioned that your wife hid things in the flower garden. I wanted to ask if that was true. And if those items would have anything to do with Lydia's death."

The man leaned forward and screwed his face up. "Sweet Emma did hide things the last year of her life. She had dementia, you know?"

I nodded.

He continued, "She would take things and secret them away as if someone wanted to steal'em." He grinned as his eyes glazed over. "She once hid our coffee scoop, of all things. It was a little yellow plastic scoop. I found it under a gnome in the backyard."

"Your coffee scoop?"

"Yep. It was mostly things like that. Not anything of value. I'm sure there are more things buried out there I just haven't missed'em yet."

I tapped my foot. "Someone told me she hid a silver comb once."

"Ah, she did! And the matching silver mirror. I found the comb, but the mirror is still missin.' Again, I don't think they would be worth a great price, though. Mostly sentimental stuff. Emma was always into the feelings."

Although the words were almost careless, Mr. Padasky said them with a great deal of feeling. *He must have loved his Emma very much. And she must have loved him because I couldn't imagine living with Mr. Padasky.*

"You told me you heard Lydia and Eben fighting the night before she died. Did you happen to overhear what it was about?" I knew the question might be another long shot. Mr. Padasky sometimes had trouble hearing.

"Just bits and pieces. I opened the backdoor and started to holler at them. But then Eben yelled something about Lydia spendin' too much time with James and not gettin' her money's worth. Then she said somethin' about just demandin' more from Regan."

"Regan? Her sister Regan?"

Mr. Padasky raised his brows at me. I could have sworn one of the white caterpillars winked at me. "How many Regans do you know, Kay? Not including the great President and actor, of course."

I nodded my head, ignoring Mr. Padasky's comments. What had Eben meant by Lydia not getting her money's worth from James? Did Eben know about Lydia's affair with her ex-husband? Where did Lydia's sister fit into this?

Maybe it was time I visited Regan Tosta.

Chapter 12

The Tosta Treasure

Regan's restaurant was located in the small town of Shallotte, North Carolina, right over the bridge from Holden Beach. I sat in my car and studied the building with its brightly colored hues of teal, orange, blue, and pink. There was something about businesses close to the beach. They looked like tourist attractions.

The Tosta Treasure was THE place in town for seafood, chicken, and steak with a family-style sit-down restaurant feel. Yet, it also had flatscreen televisions that played sports games and a small bar up front for those who wanted a drink while watching the latest game.

I walked in and immediately blended in with others on vacation. A small girl, probably barely 18, approached me with a menu. "One?" she asked.

"Oh no. I'm looking for Regan. Is she in today?"

The girl looked me up and down. "Um, let me see if she has come in yet."

I watched as she disappeared into the back. I knew of Regan, but I didn't know her personally. She was older than me, so we hadn't gone to school together, and she lived in Shallotte to be near her business. I could only hope she wasn't like Lydia.

A beautiful woman with long blonde hair, a short floral dress, and a pair of white espadrille wedges came walking toward me. She put her hand out, and I noticed her manicured acrylic nails. "Hello! I'm Regan. How can I help you?"

I swallowed as I shook her hand. Except for the long hair, Regan was the spitting image of Lydia.

"Hi, I'm Kay Wellington. I work at the same pharmacy as James, Lydia's husband. I mean, ex-husband. I wanted to ask you a few questions about your sister."

A glimmer of something passed over Regan's eyes as she dropped her hand from mine. "You were a friend of Lydia's?"

"No. I wouldn't say that. I am a friend of James'."

At that, the woman laughed, throwing her head back and her hair swinging against her hips. "Of course you are! James is the sweetest! Come into my office so we can talk."

I followed her down a darkened hallway to a black door that read Office in white calligraphy. "I haven't spoken to James yet. I've been too busy." Regan opened the door and motioned for me to sit in a white wicker chair. She walked around the black desk until she could see me. "I know the police were questioning him."

"Who is handling Lydia's arrangements?" I asked.

"Me. I already have everything done, but the authorities haven't released her body yet." She sat down in a plush white leather computer chair.

I studied the woman's face. There wasn't a single tear. Her voice didn't crack. Instead, she had a calm, polite smile on her face.

"Were you and Lydia close?"

She shook her head and for a moment, looked sad. "No. Not at all. My sister did things for herself. We rarely spoke unless she wanted something."

"Like what?"

My question got her attention, and she cocked her head at me. "Why are you asking all of these questions?"

"I want to help clear James' name. He would never hurt Lydia, much less kill her. I'm trying to figure out who did."

Regan frowned. "My sister rubbed people the wrong way. I'm sure the suspect list is long and keeping the police busy. Of course, it may have been a robbery."

"No one has mentioned anything missing."

Regan waved her hand, dismissing the thought. "I'm just guessing. But you are right. James never had the guts to stand up to Lydia. He would always back down and give her what she wanted. I felt sorry for him when they married." She took a long drink of water from a bottle on the desk.

I wasn't sure what to say. I was an only child, but weren't sisters usually closer than this?

"Someone told me Lydia had a stake in your restaurant. That she was a silent partner."

Regan's gaze met mine again, her expression dark. "When I approached the bank about my business idea, I had done all my homework. I had a business plan, a model, projections, everything. But the bank said I would need a co-signer before they would loan me the money to get started. I asked Lydia."

She dropped her gaze as she ran a nail over a corner of the desk. "Somehow, Lydia thought that meant that she co-owned The Tosta Treasure with me. She demanded half. I told her that wasn't doable because I barely made enough to live on myself as the restaurant grew. Plus, I have to budget well to keep the place running in the offseason and keep my regular employees. So, I started giving her half of my income from here."

"Did you tell the police that?" I asked slowly.

Regan jerked her head up at me. "I told Detective Cornell about Lydia's demands but not about giving her half my income. That would make me look like I had a reason to off my sister. But I would never physically hurt her. She was my only sister, my only sibling! No, I would never!"

Regan raised her voice. It was the first emotion I'd seen from her involving her sister's death. But was she emotional about her sister's death or getting blamed for her murder?

"Who do you think did it?"

Regan took another drink of water and seemed to calm down a bit. "I would check with her no-good boyfriend."

"Eben?"

"That's the one. Did you know she's brought him in here several times, and he has flirted with my servers? He even hit on me?"

My eyes grew wide, although I should have expected that. I'd met Eben. "When did he hit on you?"

"About two weeks ago. They came in to eat for free. Lydia didn't believe she had to pay for anything since she "co-owned" the place." Regan shrugged as if releasing the tension, then continued, "I told the server to wait on them and to bring me the bill when they left. I would take care of it. I was back here working when Eben knocked on my door. I told him to come in, but then he shut the door behind him. He started telling me how beautiful I am and yada, yada, yada." She waved her hand. Apparently, she got hit on a lot.

"What did you do?"

"Have you seen him? His eyes kind of pin you where you are. I recovered quickly and told him to get out. That he was disrespecting my sister and me. Do you know what he said?"

I shook my head. I had no idea.

"He said that Lydia didn't mind sharing! Can you believe that? I told him to get out of my restaurant, or I would throw him out myself. I guess he got the hint because the server came back a few minutes later with the bill and said they had left - after picking up $120 worth of food from carry-out."

"Did you tell Lydia any of this?"

Regan shook her head. "No. Lydia knew what she was getting into dating a man like Eben. She gave up James for guys like that."

"I take it you approved of James," I said softly.

Regan took a deep breath as she nodded. "James would have been good to my sister forever. He's reliable, self-controlled, even-tempered, and provides. But my sister wanted danger and wild times. Lydia let a good guy go."

The way Regan's eyes and voice softened, I began to wonder if Regan had loved her brother-in-law.

"You said you don't talk to James?"

"Not in a very long time. Lydia could be...jealous."

"But she and James have been divorced for a year."

"I know, but she could still be territorial, which is why what Eben said didn't make any sense. Why would Lydia share a guy?"

I swallowed to keep from telling Regan about Lydia's affair with James while also seeing Eben.

"I think Eben is into some stuff. Maybe illegal stuff." Regan's eyes darkened again as she studied me. "Maybe drugs."

"No one has mentioned it. What makes you think that?" I asked.

"Lydia always spoke about Eben's business dealings. Yet, I heard he only works part-time at the grocery store."

"Did Lydia say what those business dealings were?"

"No. I made a snide comment about them one day, and she closed up about it and accused me of being jealous. Sorry, but I would rather wait *years* for a stable guy than jump at the first blue-eyed demon that winked at me."

I nodded. *A stable guy? Like James?* I would *not* voice that out loud. But for some reason, her comment made me want to call Pierce. Now seemed as great a time as any.

Chapter 13

The Mosstree Cafe

I stepped out of The Tosta Treasure and into a storm. That was the only way to describe it. Huge dark clouds rolled in from the ocean, and the wind demanded the palm trees bow down to it. I made a mad dash to my Trailblazer and hopped inside, water sloshing all over the interior and coating my glasses. I would need to drive home and change clothes. I fished in my glove compartment for a few napkins and wiped my flip-flops and feet dry.

Once I found my way back onto the highway, I called Pierce.

"Kay, are you all right? There's a lot of background noise."

"Yeah, I'm fine. I'm driving through a storm."

"Where? It's not raining here."

I bit my lower lip. If I told him Shallotte, would he guess I'd spoken to Regan? "I decided to spend the morning at Holden Beach." Technically, I had been across the bridge from Holden, but close enough.

"Holden Beach? You weren't over that way to talk to Regan Tosta, were you?"

I stared at the screen on my dashboard with Pierce's name and number across it. How the heck did he know that? I needed to veer this conversation down another path and into space. "Are you busy? Want to have brunch with me?"

Pierce was quiet for a moment. "I would like that, Kay. How about that little cafe on Main Street?"

"The Mosstree Cafe?"

"That's the one, I think. The one with the painted oak on the front."

"That's it. I can meet you there in about an hour. I need to change clothes." I silently congratulated myself on diverting Pierce's attention.

However, an hour and fifteen minutes later, I sat at a small table near the front window at The Mosstree Cafe, staring into Detective Pierce Cornell's chocolate brown eyes as he repeated his question.

"Kay, did you speak to Regan Tosta this morning?"

I played with the crumble topping on my triple-berry cobbler with my fork. The Mosstree Cafe was a local establishment run by a sweet woman named Alma Mae. My parents had been bringing me here for as long as I could remember. I glanced up at Pierce. He was still waiting for my answer.

"I *may* have stopped by The Tosta Treasure."

Pierce groaned.

"Well, before you get all 'don't-be-meddling-in-police-work,' I should tell you what Regan confessed to me."

That seemed to get Pierce's attention. He leaned forward and placed his forearms on the table. He'd rolled up the sleeves of his dress shirt when he arrived. It was going to be another scorcher of a day. And now I couldn't stop staring at his arms. What was wrong with me? I played with the hem of my maybe-too-short red cotton dress and pulled my hair back into a bun.

"Kay?" Pierce waved his hand in front of my face causing me to blink. "Kay, what did Regan say to you? Something she didn't tell me?"

I pushed my glasses up my nose. "I don't guess she did. She told me that Eben hit on her a couple of weeks ago when he was with Lydia. She didn't tell her sister, but Eben alluded that Lydia would be fine sharing him."

Pierce frowned.

"She also said that Lydia demanded half of the profits from The Tosta Treasure, but there was no way Regan could do that and stay operational. So she's been paying Lydia half of her own income from the restaurant."

At that, Pierce's eyes widened. "Did she say how much? That might explain how Lydia could pay her bills and still be the life of the party without a job. She was living well between the money she received from her ex-husband and the money from her sister, plus James covering so many of her assets. We have analysts looking into her accounts now."

I swallowed a bite of cobbler. I really should have chosen a sugar-free version. This stuff was so good. "Does Regan have an alibi?"

"She was on her way to the restaurant. She says she was running late because of errands. However, she does have a printed receipt from the bank where she made her car payment." Pierce took a bite of his omelet.

"Could she have driven to Lydia's house, shoved her sister into the newel post, and then driven to the restaurant in time?"

He swallowed. "It's possible. Of course, Eben could have done it too. He says he was at his apartment until his work shift but could have double-backed to the house on foot and killed her. Or, he could have slipped out the back door at the Locklyn Market long enough to do it. Mr. French said that Eben disappears a lot during his shift."

This was not narrowing it down any. "Any news on Mr. Padasky's shovel?"

Pierce lowered his voice, his eyes darting around the almost empty cafe. "It's not Lydia's blood."

"So, he did hit a raccoon?"

Pierce nodded as he took another bite. "Guess so. It makes me rethink the cranky old dodger. I wonder if he could be more dangerous than Eben." He winked at me.

"I stopped by his place early this morning."

Pierce stopped chewing, alarm suddenly replacing the humor in his gaze. "You stopped by Eben's?"

"Eben's? No, Mr. Padasky's house. James told me that Emma Padasky hid things in her flower beds before she died. He believed they might have been expensive items. Mr. Padasky downplayed it, but someone *was* digging in his flower bed. That's why he called you. What if that person thinks there is something valuable hidden in the backyard? What if Lydia saw that person, and they panicked?"

Pierce tapped his finger on the table. "Mr. Padasky said those were nice items she buried but virtually worthless. What if Lydia knew of the buried items but didn't know their value? If James knew things were buried out back, then she probably did too. Maybe it was Lydia who was digging in the beds?"

"But you said Mr. Padasky reported someone digging around *after* Lydia's death."

"True. We just don't know yet." He set his fork down and reached for my hand. A slight current sped up my arm at his touch, my cheeks heating. "I would feel better if you stopped asking my suspects questions. Let me handle Mr. Padasky and Eben. And Regan."

"But you can't be everywhere at once. I'm not hurting anyone. I'm just helping to clarify a few things." I shrugged and gave him my broadest smile.

Pierce lowered his gaze and then peered up at me as he squeezed my hand. "I know. But you might inadvertently obstruct. Then you would be in a world of trouble. Plus, the chief said-"

"Oh, my goodness! Look who is here for brunch this morning! Lil Miss Kay Wellington!" A woman's voice rang out across the cafe, and I jumped. Louisiana-born and bred Alma Mae came around the counter, slinging a dish towel over her shoulder. "Delores! Bring Kay a caramel latte." Her dark eyes landed on Pierce's hand, holding mine across the table. "And who do we have here? I don't think we've met. I'm Alma Mae. I own this establishment."

Pierce immediately let go of my hand and shook Alma Mae's outstretched one. He introduced himself as *Detective* Pierce Cornell. Alma Mae's eyes grew as wide as the saucer on the table. She touched her hand to her chest. "Oh, my. Is this about Lydia McKellan? That poor woman."

*Do not snort in derision, Kay. The woman is dead, and that would **not** be nice.*

"I'm investigating that case, yes. But I can't talk about it," Pierce answered very matter-of-factly. I wasn't sure why I was suddenly so proud of him. We weren't even dating.

On the other hand, maybe it was because he was so gosh darn good-looking, and he was eating at my table. I was finally sitting at the cool kids' table.

"Kay, how are your parents? And poor James?"

I was pretty sure Alma Mae had heard the rumor about James possibly giving Lydia the wrong medication and the police questioning him, but she was one of the sweetest women in town.

"James is doing all right. He's at work today. Mom and Dad are well."

Alma Mae patted me on the back. "Well, you take care of them. They are good people, the Wellingtons." She said the last bit to Pierce, then added, "But you know what? I know this is none of my business, but I saw that boy Lydia allowed over to her house at nights in here the day she died."

Pierce turned almost entirely around in his chair. "Eben Reitz? Are you saying you saw Eben Reitz in here the day Lydia died? Are you sure it was him? What was he doing?"

Alma Mae studied the ceiling as if waiting for the answer to fall from the tiles. I glanced up to make sure nothing was hanging up there. "Oh, it was him, all right. He ordered a BLT, but she paid for it."

"She? Do you mean Lydia? Lydia was here?" I asked. No one had said anything about Lydia and Eben eating at The Mosstree Cafe that morning. Not even Eben.

"Lydia?" Alma Mae whispered, "Oh, no. It was her sister. Regan was having breakfast with Eben the day you found Lydia dead."

Chapter 14

Making Up is Half the Fun

Pierce and I stood outside The Mosstree Cafe next to my car. I leaned against the driver's side door. "Why would Regan have breakfast with Eben? Why wouldn't she tell me that? Instead, she acted like she despised the man."

Pierce shrugged. "That's the thing about suspects in a homicide investigation, Kay. Most of them have their own dark secrets. They only tell the police just enough information to divert attention from them." He stepped closer. "Another reason I would like you to stop speaking to these people. At least, until we have someone in custody."

I sighed, keenly aware of how close Pierce stood before me. "I can avoid Eben and probably Regan since I never encounter them. But Mr. Padasky, I see all the time at the pharmacy."

"Then just be professional. Meaning, do not go to his house to visit or snoop around." He touched a wayward hair that had managed to pull free from my messy bun. "Let me do my job."

"So, are you going to question Regan as to why she was seen eating breakfast with her sister's boyfriend only hours before her sister was murdered?"

Pierce frowned. "I am. What are you planning to do for the day?"

"Nothing." I shrugged. "Probably pick up some groceries for the week and retreat to my little she-shed-reading-nook for the rest of the day."

He smiled. "That sounds nice. Maybe I can stop by after work this evening? Is that okay?"

I returned his smile. "I would like that. Should I make us some dinner?" I tried to hide the hope in my voice.

Brunch and dinner with Pierce all on the same day? Yes, please.

"I'll call you if I can get away on time. If I can, I'll pick us up some carry-out. I saw a barbeque place a few blocks from here. Do you like pulled pork?"

"Love it."

"Okay. I'll call you later then." Pierce smiled down at me, then turned and headed for his car.

As I climbed into my Trailblazer, excitement running through me, I pulled out my phone to look at my grocery list. Usually, I would go to Food Park. But today, I figured a trip to the Locklyn Market was in order. If Pierce planned to follow up on the lead on Regan, maybe I could follow the one on Eben.

I grabbed a shopping cart - which my mother called a buggy - from the front of the Locklyn Market and began shopping the perimeter of the store. All the while, I searched for Eben. Was he not working today? I scanned the registers, the produce section, the dairy section, and the butcher shop. No Eben. Perhaps he was in the back. He probably stocked the store.

As I grabbed an apple pie from the bakery - just in case Pierce did stop by after work - I noticed Mr. French behind the customer service counter looking over a clipboard. I smiled as I approached the counter, but he didn't seem to notice me.

I stopped the cart in front of the counter and cleared my throat. He still didn't look up.

"Um, excuse me, Mr. French?"

The broad man glanced up, then broke out into a grin. "Kay Wellington! It's good to see you! Do you need help finding anything?" He set the clipboard on the counter and leaned over, his black handlebar mustache reminding me of a villain from a cartoon. I expected him to start twisting the ends very soon and laughing maniacally.

"I'm still shopping. But I was wondering if Eben is working today?"

Mr. French sneered at me. He literally *sneered* at me. "Oh, Kay. You do not want to have anything to do with that boy. He's bad news. And you are..." he trailed off.

"I'm?"

Mr. French waved his hand, almost apologetically. "Well, you're a good girl. Eben Reitz is not the type of guy you should hang around with. But if you really want to know, Eben didn't show up for work this morning."

"Do you know why? I mean, did he give you a reason?"

"Kay-"

"It's not like that, Mr. French. I had some questions for Eben about Lydia McKellan, that's all. I'm not dating him."

Mr. French seemed to consider my words as he scrunched his mouth up into a tiny little O. "Eben was a no call/no show today. He's never done that before, but maybe Lydia's death has finally gotten to him. She was a real piece of work, always bossing everyone around."

"Sounds like you had a run-in with her," I said.

Mr. French straightened. "I would overhear her barking commands to Eben when she would come into the store. Telling him what to do, how to dress, who he could talk to. You know? Lydia McKellan had an image she wanted to project."

I nodded. That sounded like Lydia. "Did Eben ever say anything back to her?"

The man gave a derisive laugh. "Yes, all the time. Eben gave as much as Lydia did. Maybe that's why she liked him. He was so unlike her ex, James. Although I must say, Eben and Lydia seemed to care for one another."

I leaned back on my heels. "How did you come to that conclusion? Sounds like they fought all the time."

Mr. French leaned over the counter again at me, that sneer back on his hairy lips, and whispered, "Kay, my girl, one of these days, you're going to learn that making up is half the fun."

If that comment had come from any other person in Locklyn, I could have stomached it. Even Mr. Padasky. But hearing the words from the comic villain's mouth made my stomach hurl.

"Oh, okay. Thanks, Mr. French!" I hurriedly backed away and swung my cart down the closest aisle. I needed to finish my shopping. Maybe after I put away the groceries at home, I would drive to Eben's apartment.

My stomach tightened again. Pierce would not be happy if I went to Eben's apartment. Of course, he probably wouldn't like it if he knew I'd come to the Locklyn Market under false pretenses, but at least it was a public place.

No. I would go home and put away the groceries. Then I would make a big pitcher of iced tea and spend the rest of the day reading a cozy mystery in my shed.

Anything to get my mind off *this* mystery.

I put away the groceries, made a pitcher of iced tea, and baked a small ziti entree in the microwave. It was late afternoon by the time I was ready to carry my tea and ziti to the she-shed-reading nook in my backyard.

I loved this place. The construction was sturdy, and I had taken the time to do an almost professional job on the paint and trim. The rocker on the little front porch completed the look. The place was even climate controlled. I'd spared no expense since I didn't have a mortgage payment hanging over my head. It was my happy place.

Carefully, I balanced my plate of ziti and glass of tea as I made my way down my back porch steps and across the yard to the shed. I kept the building locked, although I doubted anyone would break in and steal my books; then again, you never knew what people were thinking. I managed to pull the key from the lanyard and insert it into the lock, then used my hip to push the door wide.

I started to step inside when the sight registered. I vaguely heard the crash of the plate and glass as they hit the hard wooden floor. Instead, I reached for my cell in my back pocket. Without looking at the numbers, I dialed 9-1-1.

Eben Reitz lay across my green velvet chaise with a dagger protruding from his chest.

Chapter 15

One Big Mistake (Hopefully)

The police arrived only minutes after my call.

Pierce had an officer escort me inside to my living room and as far away from the scene as possible. The curb in front of my house and my carport and lawn were riddled with police cars, an ambulance, and even a fire truck. I wasn't sure why there was a fire truck, but I audibly groaned when I saw two news vans parking down the street and camera crews racing toward the house.

I lowered myself onto the couch. I needed to calm down and figure this out. None of it made sense. Why was Eben in my shed? How did he get in there? The door had been locked. I'd used the key. The building had small windows. Could he have fit in through one of those? Even if he had, he wouldn't have stabbed himself in the chest with a dagger.

"Kay." Pierce stood above me. "Are you okay?" He sat down on the coffee table, facing me.

I nodded, pushing my glasses up my nose. "I think so. I just don't get it. How did Eben get in there? The door was locked."

"You unlocked the door when you got home?" he asked, a frown forming across his brow.

"Yes. I put away the groceries, then made lunch. I carried it outside to the building and unlocked the door. That's when I spotted Eben on the chaise."

"Where do you normally keep the key to the building?"

"By the back door in the laundry room. There is a hook on the wall where I keep the lanyard with the key. It was hanging there when I got home."

"Does anyone else have a copy? Maybe you gave it to someone? The electrician, maybe?"

I shook my head. "I'm the only one with the key."

Chief Sanders came through the kitchen into the living room; a deeper frown than Pierce's crossed his face. "Kay, you all right, girl?"

I nodded.

He paused next to Pierce and studied him briefly before addressing me again. "Kay, I hate to do this, but I'm requesting that Detective Cornell take you to the station for further questioning."

"Why?" Pierce and I asked in unison. The detective stood. It was apparent Pierce had no idea what his boss was thinking.

Chief Sanders eyed me while nodding his head and waving Pierce off. "Kay, Lydia McKellan was given the wrong medication at *your* pharmacy. *You* found her dead. *You've* been seen skulking around George Padasky's place, and someone just told me they saw *you* at the Locklyn Market a few hours ago, where Eben Reitz worked. Now you have found another dead body. Eben's body in *your* locked shed."

"Chief, surely, you can't be-"

"I'm not asking you, Cornell. Take Kay to the station, and I'll question her when I get done here. This is a mess. I'm sorry, Kay."

This could not be happening. I was supposed to have dinner with Pierce tonight. But he'd warned me not to get involved.

I stood, my knees knocking together, but before we could move, my parents came barreling through the front door. I had no idea how they had made it past the police and the news crews.

"Katherine! Oh, thank God, you're fine!" My mother grabbed me and hugged me tightly.

Don't cry, Kay. This is all just a big mistake.

My father ran his hand over my back, probably making sure I was in one piece. Then he turned to Chief Sanders. "What do you know, Chief?"

Chief Sanders sighed. "All I know, Tom, is that your daughter is now our number one suspect."

Chapter 16

Trouble in Little Locklyn

I wish I could say the police station was light and airy and that Chief Sanders and the officers who'd seen me around town *for like forever* were friendly and understanding.

Instead, Pierce's fellow officers appeared confused.

That's okay. I was confused too. Yet, I shouldn't be. Everything the Chief mentioned made sense. If I were reading a cozy mystery or watching an episode on television, I would suspect myself.

Except I didn't do it.

Someone else murdered Lydia, then they murdered Eben and somehow left him in my building for me to find. Why? Had I been getting too close to something or someone? Obviously, I was terrible at this mystery business because I couldn't even pinpoint what I might know that would get me framed for Eben's murder.

Pierce led me into an interrogation room with one table and a chair on either side. Thank Heavens, he had not felt the need to handcuff me.

I sat in the metal chair with the 1970s mustard yellow plastic seat. "So, should I call a lawyer?"

Pierce frowned, then slowly sat opposite me in the lovely olive-green plastic chair. *Seriously, when was the last time this place was updated?*

"Your father followed us to the station. I heard him out front on the phone, and it sounded like he is calling a lawyer for you." He looked at me, his dark eyes searching my overly-wide blue ones. "Do you think you need a lawyer? Can you think of a reason why all of these things have you at the center?"

I shrugged. "I don't know. I mean, yes, I think I need a lawyer, which means I shouldn't answer your questions until they arrive. But, no, I never realized that I was at the center of these events. Pierce, I didn't hurt anyone, let alone kill someone."

Pierce nodded but seemed distant, guarded. This felt wrong. Just this morning, he had held my hand at the cafe. I'd thought maybe, just maybe, Pierce could be *the* one. Now, he could barely look at me.

The chair scraped when he stood suddenly. "Would you like a cup of water or coffee while you wait?"

Ignoring the question, I asked, "You can't be seriously believing the theory that I had something to do with Lydia and Eben's deaths?"

Pierce only stared at me silently, his jaw ticking.

"Huh," I finally said, breaking the silence and leaning back in the creaky chair. "I guess Mr. Padasky was right. Nice guys always get the blame."

"It's not like that, Kay. We have to go on evidence."

"What evidence?" I raised my voice but didn't care. "No one has mentioned my fingerprints being on Lydia's bottles. My fingerprints won't be on the dagger that killed Eben because I'd never seen it until today. Plus, if Eben was killed today, then I have an alibi. I spent the entire day surrounded by people. I was with Regan Tosta this morning in Shallotte, had brunch with you at the cafe, then shopped at the Locklyn Market, where I spoke to Mr. French. He probably even has security cameras that will document the time."

My breath was coming rapidly now. There was no way that sweet-good-girl Kay would go down for this.

Great, now I'm referring to myself in the third person.

Pierce put his hands up as if warding off a blow. "Kay, Chief is only questioning you. I'm sure you can go home once we get to the bottom of it."

I opened my mouth to argue, but the door swung open. My father and his attorney, another man I'd known my entire life, walked into the room.

"Detective Cornell, I'm Rick Montgomery. I represent the Wellington family. Where's Chief Sanders?" Rick stood a few inches taller than Pierce despite being in his early sixties. When I was little, I'd been afraid of the man. He had a presence about him that you couldn't ignore. He was like a boulder, and from what I'd heard from Dad, Rick could smash a court case to pieces. He won most of them.

Pierce shook Rick's hand. "He's on his way."

Rick's upper lip curled. "Then we agree that you should probably leave the questions for him. I want to speak to my client alone."

Pierce's gaze darted to me, but he nodded and walked out, closing the door behind him.

Rick shrugged as he sat down opposite me. "New kid in town, huh?" he asked, referring to Pierce.

"He is," I answered quietly. "He's a friend too."

Rick stopped shuffling the papers he was pulling out of his briefcase. "Listen to me, Kay. You can be acquaintances with the police. You can be friendly and all. But do not be friends with them. You have to be careful about that. You could inadvertently say something that they will use against you later."

When I raised my eyebrows at him, he continued, "I've seen it happen too many times. Think about it. If you have shared anything about this case, your opinions or theories, with Detective Cornell, he can use that against you."

I started to protest, but my father interrupted. "He's right, Kay. It would be better if you keep things to yourself right now." He got down on one knee to look me in the eye. I could see the worry and fear behind his gaze. "You need to do exactly what Rick tells you to do. Katherine, this is serious. We know you didn't do anything, but someone wants you to take the blame."

I blinked, fighting back the tears. "Someone thinks I'm on to them. I just wish I knew who."

Chapter 17

Time to Get Serious

D ad drove me home, where Mom was waiting and cleaning up after the officers and investigators left. Not that there was much to clean up other than dirt tracked into the house. I think Mom just wanted something to do to keep her mind off the accusations hurled at her only daughter by the Locklyn Police Department.

"So?" Mom asked after she'd turned off the vacuum in the living room. "What happens now?"

"We wait," Dad answered. "Rick is working on it. But, other than circumstance, the police have no evidence that Katherine did anything to Eben or Lydia."

Mom asked a few more questions, but I tuned her out as I went into my bedroom and shut the door. I kicked off my shoes and then fell backward onto the bed. I felt betrayed. I'd grown up in this town. I knew everyone. Yet, people were willing to speculate to the police about why I had been at the Locklyn Market. Chief Sanders, a man I'd known since I was a baby, practically accused me of the crimes.

And Pierce?

Pierce had left the interview room when Rick arrived and never came back. I didn't see him before I left either.

I guessed that what little relationship was budding between Pierce and myself was crushed under the weight of these accusations. It wasn't fair.

I sat up in bed. Someone knew I was getting close. I didn't know I was, but I must be close to whoever killed Lydia. So, the next question was, why did this person kill Eben?

Had Eben discovered what happened to Lydia? Had he suspected someone? I still didn't know why Eben and Regan had breakfast together the morning of the murder. I needed to know, now more than ever. There was no way I would allow someone to pin any of this on me. Someone was underestimating lil ole Kay Wellington with her glasses and books.

I am my grandmother's namesake. I am Katherine Wellington. I will fight for justice for Lydia and Eben, justice for James, and justice for myself. They want to see anger? I'm about to show them all some righteous anger.

I pulled an off-shoulder black jumper and a pair of espadrille wedges out of my closet. I quickly dressed, then emerged from the bedroom. Mom and Dad were still talking in hushed tones on the couch.

"Kay? Where are you going?" Mom asked.

"To the bathroom," I answered, heading toward the back of the house.

"I can see that! I mean, why are you dressed up? Surely, you are not going somewhere with all of this happening."

I took a deep breath before slowly exhaling in front of the bathroom door. "I'm fine, Mom. Honest. I just need to shake this off and go out for a while."

"Out where? Tom, talk some sense into your daughter."

I stepped into the bathroom and shut the door before Dad could give his two cents. They were both being protective, and I couldn't fault them for that, but this was something I needed to do. I was the one someone was trying to frame for not one but two murders in town.

I washed my face, reapplied my makeup, and then brushed my hair until it fell onto my shoulders in dark waves. I stared at my reflection in the mirror. The black eyeliner made my blue eyes pop. Finally, I slipped on my glasses.

My first stop? Miss Regan Tosta at the Tosta Treasure. Pierce had probably already interviewed her, but I planned to do more than ask her questions. If Regan was behind framing me for murder, she better get ready for a fight.

It was time to get serious.

I pulled up to the Tosta Treasure just in time to see Regan bolting out the front door to her car. The way her face was screwed up, I guessed she was in a panic. I jumped out of my car and reached her driver's side door before she could open it.

"I take it you heard about Eben?" I asked, leveling my gaze with hers. She was taller than me, more like Lydia, but the seriousness of what someone was doing to me had given me the courage I didn't know I possessed.

Regan pulled her hand away. "Um, yes, I did. It's horrible." Her eyes grew wide. "I heard Eben was found in your shed."

"He was, which is why I need you to answer some questions."

Regan exhaled. "Kay, I don't think I can help you. I've already told the police everything."

"Why were you having breakfast with Eben the day Lydia died?"

Regan's posture suddenly slumped as she leaned against her car. "Detective Cornell asked about that too."

I motioned for Regan to sit on a concrete bench near the restaurant. She lowered her head as she took a seat beside me. "Regan, what did you tell Detective Cornell?"

"I told him that Eben and I met weekly for breakfast. We have been doing that for months."

"Why? Did Lydia know?"

Regan shook her head, her thick blonde hair brushing around her shoulders. "No. Lydia would have had a fit."

"So why?" I pushed my glasses further up my nose as if seeing Regan better would somehow make all this make sense.

Regan covered her mouth with both hands as she looked into the distance. She blinked rapidly, fighting back the tears. "I told you that Lydia demanded money from me for what she considered her part of the business, right? I paid her a sum out of my own income. Eben knew about it. He was skimming some of that money away from Lydia and giving it back to me."

I leaned away from Regan. "Eben was stealing from Lydia?"

"Not really stealing," Regan sniffed out. "It was my money. He just found a way to get the money back. Well, most of it, anyway."

My mind reeled. Regan could have wanted her sister dead to keep from having to pay her the money Lydia thought she was owed. Other than a receipt from making her car payment, Regan may have had enough time to get to Lydia's home, kill her, and then go to the restaurant. Eben had found a way to return some of the money to Regan. Had Regan considered Eben a loose end? I surveyed the semi-busy parking lot. At least there were people around.

"Who do you think killed Eben?" I asked.

Did you do it?

"Anyone, I suppose. You either loved him or hated him."

"Which one were you? You acted like you couldn't stomach him when we spoke before."

Regan shrugged. "I didn't hate him, but I wasn't one of his exes."

"One of his exes?"

"Eben was a love'em and leave'em kind of guy. I'm sure he would have left Lydia eventually. Sometimes when he and I were having breakfast, he would get a call from this girl. I think her name was Sally. Anyway, I could hear her screaming at him over the phone."

"Why?"

"I don't know. I asked Eben, and he only remarked that she was bitter because he'd left her for Lydia."

I stretched my legs out in front of me. "One more question. What did Eben want from you? He didn't seem like the type of guy to give something without wanting something in return. He found a way to get your money back from your sister in exchange for what, exactly?"

Regan rolled her eyes over to me. "He wanted to use my boathouse in the canal."

Chapter 18

The Houseboat

I had never been to a boathouse before, but Regan's was not what I expected. I pulled into the lot near the docks, then followed the arrows to find her gray prefabricated boat house. It was rectangle-shaped with a cute outdoor kitchen and a small bunkhouse. I pulled the key Regan had given me from my pocket.

Regan had shared with Pierce why she'd been seen having breakfast with Eben. But she had not confided to him why Eben had been so gracious to steal from Lydia to return money to Regan. Also, I didn't think Pierce knew of Eben's ex-girlfriend, Sally. Maybe she was jealous and angry and decided to get rid of her ex and Lydia.

For some reason, Eben wanted access to Regan's boathouse, which she rarely used. I turned back toward the door to the bunkhouse and felt the walkway shift. I didn't think I could ever stay on one of these. What did Regan do during hurricane season?

I slid the key into the lock, then pushed the door open. The bunkhouse was a little cramped, with a twin-size bed perched against the wall in what seemed like the perfect-sized nook. A blue and pink oriental rug was the only luxury item in the room. The window above the bed was magnificent but the only window in the room. It was a neat and clean space. Although Regan rarely spent any time down here, the boathouse was immaculate. I ran my hand over the built-in book shelving and peeked inside the drawers installed on one wall. Nothing out of the ordinary; some clothes, beauty accessories, flashlights, and a couple of paperbacks.

I sat down on the bed. Why did Eben want to use this boathouse? Surely, he had a reason. It didn't appear like he used it for parties - it was too clean. I mulled the questions around in my head for a few minutes. Maybe I should ask some of Regan's boathouse neighbors if they saw Eben with anyone or doing anything strange.

I stood and started for the door when the toe of my espadrille wedge sandal caught on the oriental rug, and I fell forward. I barely caught myself before my face planted into the floor.

Great, at least I didn't break my glasses. That was one expense I didn't need right now. But as I pulled myself up, thankful no one had seen my klutzy move, something shiny caught my eye.

Sticking out from the corner of the mattress was the end of a bracelet.

I crawled closer to the bed, pulled on the shiny object, and watched in awe as a diamond tennis bracelet landed in my palm. Was this Regan's bracelet?

I stood, ripped the blanket, pillows, and sheets from the bed, and tossed them onto the floor. Then with all my strength, I flipped the mattress away from the wall. My mouth gaped open.

Lying on the box spring were bundles of cash, piles of jewelry, and little bags of white powder.

I exhaled as I pulled out my cell and called Pierce's number.

Chapter 19

Busted by a Handsome Detective

A s soon as the phone began to ring, I disconnected the call and slid the phone back into my pocket.

What am I doing?

The police had all but accused me of Lydia and Eben's murders. So now, here I was, standing in this boathouse full of cash, drugs, and, most likely, stolen jewels. My fingerprints were all over the shelves and drawers and the tennis bracelet.

I exhaled again. *Oh God, what do I do?*

Who is going to believe that I didn't have anything to do with this? Maybe Regan could vouch for me since she'd given me the key. Then again, if Regan had something to do with Lydia and Eben's deaths, I played straight into her hand.

I was terrible at this amateur sleuthing thing. They always made it look easy on television and in books.

I looked around the room. Had anyone seen me enter the boathouse? Could I wipe my prints off everything?

I dropped the mattress with a thud, then raked my hands through my hair. What the crap was I thinking?! I would wipe away whomever else's prints were here too. I pulled the phone out again. Could I trust Pierce? Should I call Rick? Maybe Rick was the better person to call. He could just about get anyone out of a jam.

A sudden bang on the door made me jump. My heart sped up to an impossible rate as I looked down at the cash and jewels and drugs. This could not end well.

"K ay? Are you in there?" Pierce's voice came through the door.

I wanted to call out, but instead, I stared at the incriminating evidence before me as if it already had my name on it.

"Kay? Regan said she gave you the key. And I can see your car parked from here. Kay?" Pierce tried the doorknob.

Regan told him I was here and she'd given me the key. Maybe not all was lost.

Maybe.

I took a deep breath, crossed the room, and cracked open the door. Pierce stood on the opposite side, tall and perfect, with those chocolate brown eyes staring at me imploringly.

"Hey, you know you really shouldn't be here," he said.

"Don't I know it," I mumbled as I stepped back to allow him entry.

His mouth gaped as he viewed the bedding on the floor and the mattress, now half off the bed. "What on earth?" He turned to me. "Did you touch anything?"

I swallowed hard at the seriousness in his voice. "Just...everything," I admitted. "Well, everything except for the money, jewelry, and those bags of powder. I did touch this." I handed him the bracelet.

Pierce sighed as he removed an evidence bag from somewhere inside his suit jacket. "I'll need you to start from the beginning, Kay."

I filled Pierce in on everything Regan had told me and how I found the hidden items. I left out the part about me falling on the floor. I still had some dignity left.

Pierce drew closer to the bed as he began snapping pictures of the items lying on the boxsprings with his phone. "So you lifted the mattress and found these?"

"Yes. I don't think Regan left them here."

Pierce frowned. "More than likely, Eben did."

"Regan mentioned to me that she believed that Eben was involved in drugs. I guess this proves that she was right. Do you think someone he was dealing with killed him?"

Pierce put his phone up to his ear, listening to it ring. "Maybe," he answered me before turning his attention to the voice on the other end of the line. He was calling in the discovery. I could only pray that the Chief would see I had nothing to do with this. I wasn't even aware that the boathouse existed until Regan mentioned it.

When Pierce disconnected his call, I asked, "So Eben was using this place to make deals and hide stuff, right?"

"Looks like it," he answered, scrolling through the pictures on his phone.

"Pierce, I didn't do anything to Eben and Lydia."

His gaze lifted to mine, then he bit his lower lip. "I never believed that you did, Kay. The Chief has to rule you out, that's all."

"Does this rule me out? I didn't know about this place until Regan told me that Eben wanted to use it."

Pierce inhaled. "As far as I am concerned, you are innocent. But you really should have called me when she told you about it. You cannot go into places by yourself trying to be a detective. That's what got you into this mess from the start."

I dropped my gaze from his. He was right. I was in trouble with the Chief because I'd wanted to find out who killed Lydia since I knew it wasn't James.

"Hey," Pierce said softly, bringing me back to the present moment. "Let's go outside and wait for the crew. I need to run this by Chief Sanders. If it's all right with you, when I'm done, maybe I can follow you back to your place? Make sure you're okay?"

I studied the handsome detective, who stood several inches taller than me. I couldn't think of a better way to end this horrible day.

"Yes. I would like that very much, Pierce."

Chapter 20

The Note

But my joy was short-lived.

I parked under my carport but waited to climb out until Pierce pulled up in front of my house. I hoped he was planning on coming inside instead of driving away. Relief flooded through me when he turned off the engine and got out, peeling his suit jacket off and tossing it into the back seat, then rolling his shirt sleeves up his forearms.

I half-smiled at him as he joined me on the walk. I could order us a pizza. With my eventful day, the last thing I wanted to do was cook. My thoughts stayed on mozzarella until I realized there was a piece of paper stuck in my screen door. I glanced up at Pierce.

"Are you expecting something?" he asked, eyeing the note.

"I don't think so. It looks like Mom and Dad have already left. Maybe it's from them." I opened the door and snatched the paper before it could fall onto the porch. It was a piece of red construction paper folded in half. I carefully opened it to see letters from a black permanent marker.

Kay,

You should have left well enough alone. Now Eben is dead, and it is all your fault. Leave things be, or you're next.

"Stay here. Don't move," Pierce said as he scrambled back toward his car. A moment later, he returned with an evidence bag and a large set of plastic tweezers. I watched as he carefully slid the open letter into the evidence bag.

"Someone killed Eben because I got too close. They must think I know who it is."

Pierce was already on the phone, calling in this new discovery to the chief. He motioned to the front door. "Let's go inside and out of the public eye."

I didn't bother pointing out that none of my neighbors were outside. I guess they could be watching through the windows. I opened the door, and Pierce followed me inside.

"Do you think any of my neighbors noticed someone putting that note in the door?" I asked as Pierce finished his call and walked through my house, checking in closets and under the bed for an intruder.

"I'll start knocking on some doors. But this," he raised the plastic-encased letter in the air as he spoke, "is a threat on your life. You obviously didn't leave it here. This tells me that someone else killed Lydia and Eben."

I followed Pierce back through my house once he was satisfied no one was hiding in the laundry room. He motioned for me to join him on the couch. "Kay, what is it you do know?"

"What?"

"The person who sent you this note believes you are getting too close. You must know something."

I shook my head emphatically. "No, Pierce! I really have no idea."

"Tell me what you do know," he answered softly, leaning closer. I could smell the subtle hint of his cologne.

"Lydia demanded that Regan give her half the profits of The Tosta Treasure. Regan couldn't afford that and keep the place running, so she gave Lydia half her income. Eben knew about it and, somehow, got most of the money back to Regan in exchange for using her boathouse."

Pierce nodded. "We know Eben used the boathouse to store drugs, allegedly stolen jewels, and cash. It would have been difficult for Regan to have made it to Lydia's house after she made her car payment, killed her sister, and then drove to Shallotte to the restaurant. The time frame is too tight."

"So, we rule Regan out of Lydia's murder? What about Eben's?"

"She was working at the time the coroner said Eben was killed. Dozens of people saw her." Pierce's gaze held a faraway look. "What about Mr. Padasky?"

"I don't think he could physically take Eben down, do you?"

Pierce tapped his knuckles across his knee. "Eben was stabbed through the chest. It would have had to have been a surprise with great force. The coroner also stated that the attacker was taller than Eben based on the angle of the dagger. Mr. Padasky is slumped over a bit."

"And for all his mean mug, he's kind of frail," I commented.

Pierce laughed. "Mean mug? He's the sweetest man in town. He should lead the Welcoming Committee."

The image flitting through my mind of Mr. Padasky welcoming someone with a pan of brownies made me laugh too. "He did know that Lydia kept her backdoor unlocked, and everyone knew he didn't like her. But unless it was an accident and she fell down the stairs when he confronted her, I don't think he did it. Okay, so we rule out Mr. Padasky. So, who does that leave?"

"James and Miranda."

"James didn't kill Lydia. He was at work."

"I asked your father for the surveillance footage from that day. Did he tell you?"

I shook my head. Dad hadn't mentioned any of that to me. Maybe he was afraid I would worry. Or involve myself even further in this investigation.

"There are gaps in the footage."

Pierce continued when I just stared at him, "James moves off-screen several times. For long periods. The cameras don't cover every area."

"So? It's mostly just the kitchen area that it doesn't cover. It's where we compound and dilute medications. We never had a reason to add a camera there."

"It is the kitchen area, but a door off from there leads to the consultation room, yes?"

"Sure."

"And from the consultation room, you can turn right and slip into the back room. What's in the back room area?"

I shrugged, picturing the back of the store. "The back room is where we store seasonal items we don't need yet. It also has the hallway leading to the break room, bathrooms, and Dad's office."

"And the back door."

I leaned away from Pierce. "If James went out the back door, the camera would have caught him. We have surveillance covering all the doors."

Pierce raised his brows at me. "Not for that day. According to your father, the camera for the back door was down the day Lydia died."

Chapter 21

Parents Just Don't Understand

"I don't understand. Dad always checks the cameras. The footage is constantly running on the monitors in his office," I said, frowning at the note Pierce still held in the evidence bag.

"Well, those cameras were out that day. Your father said he climbed a ladder and discovered the cord was disconnected. Now either it became disconnected on its own," Pierce raised an eyebrow at that scenario before continuing, "or someone wanted to access that door without anyone seeing them."

I shook my head. "I do not believe James would kill Lydia. Does he have an alibi for Eben's murder?"

"He was at work. The cameras place him there during that time. Miranda, however, did not arrive at work until after Lydia's murder, according to the time frame the coroner gave us. Nor was she at work when Eben was killed."

"Miranda? I mean, she didn't like Lydia, and she's always liked James, but to kill his ex-wife? I don't know. And why would she kill Eben?"

"That's something I'm trying to figure out. She said she was at home during the time of both murders. Then again, she is too small to have stabbed Eben at that angle. Could be two people, I suppose." He studied the note through the plastic. "I'm going to get this over to our handwriting specialist. Maybe they can give us a profile on who wrote it." He held the bag up. "Maybe we can lift a print off it."

The thought of being someone's target and being alone caused a knot of dread to form in my stomach. I involuntarily shivered.

Pierce placed the note on the coffee table before facing me again. "Hey, are you okay?" he asked in the softest of tones.

I shrugged. "I don't know. I think so. The thought of staying here alone after the last few days is kind of scary. Maybe I should pack a bag and go to Mom and Dad's for at least a few days."

I didn't want to do that, but the more I thought about it, the better. I couldn't venture out to my reading nook/she shed either because the police still considered it a crime scene. They said I would have to call in a forensic cleaner once it was cleared.

"That would make me feel better, Kay. Why don't you pack a bag while I question some of your neighbors and see if they saw anyone leave this note? Then I'll follow you to your parents' home and make sure you get settled in, okay?"

I nodded at Pierce. He really was the most considerate man I'd ever met. Not to mention the most swoon-worthy detective on the force.

I t was the most awkward encounter I'd ever lived through *if* you didn't count Junior Prom.

Standing in my parents' living room, I watched as my mother and father surveyed and interviewed Detective Pierce Cornell. Mom asked him every embarrassing and nosy question that flitted through her mind while Dad gave him the evil eye.

This was precisely why I dated very few guys when I lived at home.

"O-kay," I interrupted Mom as she asked Pierce why he wasn't married yet. "Detective Cornell needs to get back to the station." I turned to Pierce. "Thank you for following me here. I'll be fine now."

Pierce nodded, then said his goodbyes to my parents. The looks on their faces told me this wasn't over. I was pretty sure Mom was already planning my wedding. *Parents just don't understand;* I thought and started humming the song as I followed Pierce out to the wraparound front porch.

"Thank you, Pierce. Seriously. Thanks for believing me all along."

Pierce smiled. "We'll find out who is doing this. Are you really all right to stay here?"

I nodded as a lump in my throat started to grow. He sounded so sincere and concerned about me.

"Kay, call me if you need anything or receive another message. It doesn't matter the time." He reached out and touched my arm.

Ignoring the little jolts of electricity at his touch, I smiled. "I will. I promise."

A few minutes later, I resumed my seat in the living room of the two-story farmhouse my parents called home. It was rustic, and from how my mother decorated it, people would have thought we lived during the pioneer times. Dad turned on the news, but thankfully, they covered the weather. I certainly didn't want to hear any more about the McKellan-Reitz murders.

I sank deeper into the cushions when the doorbell rang.

"I'll see who it is," Mom said, rushing out of the room.

"I hope it's not a reporter," Dad said.

"What makes you think it would be?" I asked.

"There was one nosing around your place after you left with the police. I gave the no-comment answer, and eventually, he left."

"Hmm. What station was he with?"

Dad shrugged. "I don't know, Katherine. Why would that matter?"

"It doesn't. I wondered if it was a local station or if other networks picked it up. I'd rather have the former." *Or if the man left that note on my door.*

"I agree," Dad answered softly, his eyes glued to the television.

"Look who I found on our front porch!" Mom announced as she came back into the living room. A tall, thin woman with bright red hair trailed behind her.

I gasped at the shock of seeing this woman in my parents' home. We only knew her in passing. "Mrs. French?"

"Hello, Kay. I was hoping I could speak to you. It's about Eben Reitz...and Sally."

"Sally?"

Wasn't that the name of one of Eben's ex-girlfriends, the one Regan told me about?

"Yes. Sally. My daughter."

Chapter 22

Diamonds are a Girl's Best Friend

"P lease, have a seat, Mrs. French."

The tall woman sat down rigidly on the cushion beside me. I glanced at my father. His eyes were as huge as mine. Why would Mrs. French, who owned the Locklyn Market with her husband, want to talk with me about her daughter?

Mom hurried out of the room, I assumed for coffee, tea, or some other drink. My mother oozed decorum.

"Mrs. French, I don't believe I've ever met your daughter Sally." I moved over a few inches so the woman could relax against the cushions. She bit her lower lip, and I caught her eyes darting over the living room, yet she avoided my and my father's stares.

"My husband told me that you and Eben Reitz were seeing each other," she finally said as my mother entered the room carrying a tray of glasses and a pitcher.

"Katherine? Is that true?" Mom asked.

"No. Absolutely not. But I think I know why Mr. French thought I was." I turned back to the redhead, who stared blankly at me. "I stopped by the store the other day to ask Eben a few questions about

Lydia McKellan. We were outside in the alley by the dumpster, and Eben was leaning over me as he spoke when your husband opened the back door. From his angle, it probably looked like we were together. And Eben even made a snide comment about it, but we were *not* dating. Not even close."

Mrs. French seemed to relax at my words. "Oh, that makes so much more sense," she said, sounding relieved. "My husband has a way of jumping to conclusions. I told him I thought it was nonsense. I could never see Eben dating someone like you."

I raised an eyebrow. Was that a backhanded compliment?

Mrs. French must have sensed the offense because she quickly added, "I meant to say that Eben could be a troublemaker and a womanizer. He was a flirt until he got what he wanted. And you are one of the sweetest, smartest, and quietest girls in the whole town." She waved her hand as if that explained everything.

I frowned down into the glass of iced tea Mom handed me. Did everyone feel that way about me? Maybe people thought I was too sweet, too bright, too quiet to even ask out on a date?

Mrs. French must have read my mind as she reached over and patted my hand. "Those are not bad qualities, Kay. On the contrary, those are the best qualities to have. Someone like Eben would have taken advantage of you."

I forced my lips into a tight smile, trying not to let her words affect me. Why should they? She was complimenting me, but it felt strange somehow. As if there was more between the lines, but I couldn't quite put my finger on it. I glanced over at my parents. Mom now sat on the arm of my father's chair, watching the interaction with curiosity. My father frowned.

He finally spoke. "Mrs. French? What does Kay's relationship with Eben, or lack thereof, have to do with your daughter?"

Thank you, Dad, for finally getting to the real reason why the woman is here. I looked back into Mrs. French's hazel eyes until she dropped her gaze to her lap.

"My daughter Sally got mixed up with Eben shortly after he started working for us. We cautioned her against it. Not only because he was an employee, but I'd seen him hitting on other girls. But you know how young women are," she directed this statement to Mom. "They never listen to wise advice."

Both my parents nodded in silence.

What the heck, guys? I never got into trouble the whole time I was growing up. I threw my parents an exasperated look before addressing Mrs. French.

"How old is Sally?"

"Barely twenty."

"So, she and Eben were around the same age," I commented, primarily to myself, as I remembered Pierce saying that Eben was twenty-one.

"Yes. We would have been fine with her dating him if he hadn't been a womanizer."

"How long did they date?"

"That's just it. I'm not sure. I think they dated in secret because he was seeing Ms. McKellan."

I sipped my tea and mulled this information around in my head. "What makes you think they dated at all?"

"Sally started wearing diamond jewelry I'd never seen before. Jewelry too expensive for her to afford on her own. First, it was a pair of diamond studs that she never took off. Then it was a diamond ring that she wears on the ring finger of her right hand. It has to be at least two carats. I think they were gifts from Eben."

I thought about the stolen jewels in the boathouse. "A pair of ear-rings and a ring. Did you ask her about them?"

"She said they were from a secret admirer." She rolled her eyes at this, then took a drink of her tea.

"What makes you think they were from Eben then? I wouldn't think he could afford diamonds like that. Unless you pay awfully well at the store." I smiled, trying to ease the tension. But also because no one other than the police knew about the loot found on Regan's boathouse. It wasn't public knowledge.

Mrs. French leveled her gaze with mine. "I overheard her on the phone with him. She told him she couldn't find the diamond tennis bracelet he'd given her. I think he must have yelled at her because she replied that she was going to go see Lydia, and the woman had better not be wearing it."

Chapter 23

Thelma and Louise in Locklyn?

I stared at Mrs. French. Had she just implicated her daughter in Lydia's murder?

"Did Sally go see Lydia?" I asked hesitantly, taking a drink of my tea.

Mrs. French shrugged. "I don't know. The next thing, she was on the phone with her best friend, Miranda."

Tea suddenly spewed from my mouth and onto Mrs. French, who shrieked and jumped away from me. I covered my mouth as I tried to speak, coughing tea from my lungs as the sugary drink made its way out my nose and mouth and down the wrong pipe.

"Did you say *Miranda*?" I choked out.

But Mrs. French was up and using a napkin Mom handed her to try and clean the tea, and admittedly my spit, from her tailored dress pants and white blouse. And she looked very, very angry.

I stood, trying to subtly wipe the grossness from my own face with a napkin. "Mrs. French, I'm so sorry. I didn't mean to do that. I got choked. Did you say that Sally's best friend's name is Miranda?"

The woman glanced at me, her frown indicating she was done with this visit. "Yes. Miranda Good."

So, Miranda and Sally French were best friends. Who knew? Apparently, not I.

What did this mean? Was there a connection here? I sat cross-legged on my old bed in my childhood bedroom, a room filled with bright colors and images of unicorns. My parents had gone to bed, but I had made myself a cup of coffee and grabbed Mom's unhealthiest snack - dark chocolate sea salt caramels. I needed caffeine and sugar to think this through. Healthy eating could wait a day.

According to Mrs. French, Sally was secretly seeing Eben. It sounded as if she was jealous of Lydia and was afraid that Eben had given the woman the diamond tennis bracelet. Why would she secretly have an affair with Eben knowing he was with Lydia?

My stomach twisted at the next thought. What were the chances that Sally told her best friend about her romantic relationship with Eben? My belly made a strange sound as I wondered aloud, "Did Sally and Miranda work together to rid the world of Lydia? Then maybe something happened, and they had to get rid of Eben too? Maybe their own version of ride-and-die or *Thelma and Louise*?"

But how? Eben was stabbed by someone taller than him, someone strong. Miranda was too small, like a fairy. But Sally? I had never seen Sally. Could she be tall enough? Did she have an alibi for the time of Lydia's and Eben's murders?

I grabbed my cell from the nightstand. I needed to alert Pierce to what I'd learned, but one glance at the clock told me it was too late at night. Then again, Pierce would want to know about any leads.

My finger hovered over the call icon. Another thought occurred to me. Why had Mrs. French believed I was the best person to confide in about Sally? Technically, she didn't confess, as my parents hung onto every word and even threw out their own theories after the woman left. But why come to me?

She said she thought I had a relationship with Eben. If I had been involved with Eben, why would she have told me anything about his relationship with her daughter?

Something wasn't connecting, and I couldn't put my finger on it. I'd observed Mrs. French as we talked. But maybe she was doing the same. Maybe Mrs. French had been watching my reaction to the news of Eben and her daughter's relationship.

I decided that tomorrow I would question Miranda about Sally and find the young woman myself. Then, looking over at my old bedroom closet, I frowned. Was it still there after all these years?

I crossed the room and slid the two sliding doors open to reveal an almost empty closet, save for some old formal dresses and shirts I wouldn't be caught dead in today. There, hung on a hook to the right, was my high school backpack. The leather bag looked worn now. I'd carried it all four years of high school because Dad had paid a fortune for it. Quietly, I unzipped the top and plunged my hand inside. When my palm closed over the plastic, I smiled.

Hopefully, the pepper spray was still good. If Sally killed Lydia and Eben, I needed some way to protect myself.

T he following day, I parked in front of Miranda's apartment building. Last night when I fell asleep, I had been determined to question Miranda about Eben's relationship with the woman who is the daughter of the owners of The Locklyn Market and, apparently, Miranda's best friend. But now that I was here, part of me wanted to hide.

Someone thought I was too close to this murder investigation. They had left me a note *and* a daggered Eben in my shed. What would happen if it was the team of Miranda and Sally, and I cornered them? Would I wind up in my she-shed, or would my body lie under the mattress in the boathouse until someone found me like a stolen diamond bracelet?

My hand tightened around the plastic top of the pepper spray can. I was armed. I'd worn a pair of blue palazzo pants to hide the can in the deep pockets. I adjusted my black tank top and pulled my hair back into a bun. Today was going to be another scorcher.

With a deep breath, I opened my car door. It was now or never.

But just as I slammed the door behind me, an orange extension-cab truck peeled into the parking lot, music blasting through the stereo, and slid into a parking spot a few cars from mine. The bass shook the windows of the vehicles between the truck and me. A tall woman with thick dark hair, who rivaled Regan Tosta in height and beauty, hopped out of the cab and started toward the apartment building.

She wore a floral maxidress with thin straps and looked like a woman on a mission. I raised a brow, slowing down so she wouldn't careen into me on the sidewalk. I watched her march right up to Miranda's door and wrap her knuckles hard on the wood.

I slowed down behind her. She didn't even seem to notice me. Finally, Miranda cracked the door open.

"Hey, Chicka," the woman said. "You ready to roll?"

I knew it! Thelma and Louise!

Miranda looked over Gorgeous Girl's shoulder at me, her eyes lighting up. "Kay? What are you doing here?"

Gorgeous Girl peered at me over her shoulder, studying my outfit, then turned back to her friend. "Who's she?" Her tone made me want to run and hide behind the bushes.

Snooty, much?

Miranda opened the door wider and stepped around her friend. "This is Kay Wellington. I work at her dad's pharmacy. Everything okay?" She directed the question at me.

Gorgeous Girl surveyed me again - this time with interest.

I gave her my best smile, although it was not returned. "Nothing's wrong. I was hoping to talk to you about something. Mrs. French stopped by my parents' house last night." I stared at the dark-haired woman as I spoke.

She pivoted her body towards me. "Kady French is my mother. Why would she stop by *your* parents' house?"

Wow. So this was Sally. Eben must not have been attracted to her personality. She did realize her parents just owned a grocery store, right? They weren't the Hiltons.

"Kady French is your mom? Wow, I didn't realize," I lied. "You must be Sally."

The young woman studied my face again but remained silent. *She's like an original mean girl,* I decided. I pushed on. "Your mom wanted to ask me about my relationship with Eben Reitz." I waved my hand in the air like it was no big deal.

Sally's eyes grew as wide as saucers instantly. "Your relationship with Eben?"

"Reitz. Eben Reitz. Did you know him? He - passed away - suddenly the other day."

Miranda tilted her head up at Sally as if waiting for a reaction. But Sally's gaze was locked onto mine. I could almost see the wheels turning.

"I knew him. Vaguely. He worked for my parents."

"Oh, yeah, at the market." I congratulated myself on sounding so nonchalant.

"Were you seeing him?" Sally asked.

"I didn't know you were dating anyone," Miranda piped in, looking confused.

"Not really dating," I answered, giving them both a sly smile and praying this conversation never reached my parents' ears. "Mr. French caught us out back of the store one day." I shrugged, rolling my eyes. "You know how it is."

Sally's face turned red, and I could see the anger moving down her neck and arms. She shook her head. "So you're the bimbo."

"Why do you say that?" I asked, forcing myself to remain calm. "Bimbo implies one of us was straying. You can ask Miranda. I'm not attached to anyone."

Sally took a step toward me, and it took every ounce of courage to stand rooted to the concrete. She was taller than me. So. Much. Taller.

"Eben wasn't attached to anyone either," she huffed out at me with a smirk. "Just ask Lydia McKellan."

"She's dead."

"I know."

Chapter 24

Kay vs Wonder Woman

"**Y**ou know *what*?" I asked Sally, keeping my eyes on hers while sliding my hand into my palazzo pants to grip the pepper spray can.

"That Lydia's dead. It was all over the news. But I did talk to Eben occasionally, and he told me he was seeing some stalker girl because she wouldn't leave him alone."

Um, that would be you. "I thought you said you knew him vaguely. It sounds to me like you knew him better than that."

My retort sparked anger in Sally's eyes, and she tilted her head slightly, causing the sunlight to reflect off a diamond stud in her ear. "Eben was murdered. Did you know that? Do the police know that you were seeing him?"

"I know he was murdered because his body was found in *my* back-yard shed," I answered cooly, trying to understand what Sally might be saying. If she had killed Eben and placed him there, she knew that's where the police found him. She would know exactly who I was.

But if she didn't kill Eben...

"But do the police know you were a couple?" she asked.

"Maybe we do," a deep voice cut into the conversation, and Sally, Miranda, and I turned to see Pierce standing on the sidewalk. "Or maybe we don't."

"What part of 'let me do my job, and you stay out of it,' are you not understanding?" Pierce asked, a deep frown between his brows. We sat in his car in front of Miranda's apartment building. Thankfully, I was in the front seat and not the back.

"I was going to call you last night, but it was too late."

Pierce threw me a sideways glance, clearly not believing my excuse. "And you are here. Why?"

"Why are you here?"

"Kay," his tone of voice held a warning. "You first."

I sighed. "Mrs. French, who owns The Locklyn Market, stopped by last night to ask me about Eben. Her husband had told her that he believed Eben and I had a relationship. Which you know we did *not*. Anyway, she told me that Eben had been involved with her daughter, Sally. That Amazonian," I said, gesturing toward Miranda's apartment building, "is Sally."

"Eben was seeing Sally on the side?"

"Like mashed potatoes and gravy."

Pierce stared at me, probably thinking I shouldn't try to be funny.

"Stay in the car until I get back. I mean it. I'm going to go talk to her."

I grabbed his arm. "She doesn't know that her mother told me that. Sally thinks that Eben and I-"

"Were involved. Yes, I got that from the conversation I overheard."
He looked perturbed.

"Sorry. I didn't know what else to say. I wanted to get a read on Wonder Woman."

"She's Wonder Woman now? Not the Amazonian?" He grinned.

"Wonder Woman is Amazonian. Anyway, I was calling her Gorgeous Girl in my head. How could someone who looks like Gal Gadot be so mean?"

"I didn't think she was mean."

"That's because as soon as she saw you, she melted. Look, her mother said that Sally has new diamond jewelry that Mrs. French was sure came from Eben. She's wearing a pair of earrings that I'm pretty sure are real diamonds right now."

Pierce's gaze narrowed at the apartment building. "That's interesting. Stay here."

He started to open the car door when I tugged on his arm again. "Wait. You still haven't told me why you're here?"

He sighed. "I wanted to ask Miranda some questions about her whereabouts at the time of Eben's murder. If I go now, I can ask her and this Sally."

"And you want me to sit here and wait for you?"

"Yes. Sit here, and I might tell you what I learned when I return. Maybe."

I watched Pierce cross the sidewalk and knock on Miranda's door. The blinds in the window facing the parking lot flicked open and shut, but Pierce couldn't see them from where he stood. *They're checking to see if the cop's car is still here*. Maybe they did kill Lydia and Eben and were now inside the apartment, freaking out, thinking that Pierce was onto them.

The door opened, and Miranda stuck her head out. A verbal exchange occurred between Pierce and my coworker, then Miranda opened the door wider and motioned for Pierce to come inside.

With one last look over his shoulder at me, Pierce walked inside the apartment and shut the door.

Pierce had been inside Miranda's apartment for an eternity. I was sure of it. I glanced at the clock on my phone. Okay, so it had only been twenty minutes. But what was taking him so long?

In the movies, the detectives or amateur sleuths always just confronted the bad guys, they confessed, and that was the end. Sally was tall enough to have stabbed Eben in the chest and left the dagger at that angle. She seemed pretty strong, too. She could easily have bounced Lydia's head off the newel post out of jealousy. Sally had looked like she'd wanted to bounce my head off the concrete.

Five more minutes slowly ticked by before Pierce emerged from Miranda's apartment. Alone.

He climbed into the car.

"Well?" I asked before he'd even shut the door.

"Sally was seeing Eben, but he told her he planned to break up with Lydia. He told her he was only dating Lydia to build a nest egg for them."

"Them? Eben and Sally?"

"Yeah. He gave her some jewelry to prove he loved her and her only. I told her about the stolen jewels and asked her to bring all the pieces she's received from him to the station. She's torn up about the whole thing."

I frowned but kept myself from commenting on Sally's sudden grief. She hadn't looked sad or upset earlier. "Where were Miranda and she headed?"

"I don't know. I didn't ask. Miranda was making her a cup of tea when I left."

"So what happens now?"

"We're still running the stolen items through the database looking for reports. We will add those to the list when Sally brings her pieces in. I told her not to leave town, but her alibi for the day of Eben's murder may prove true."

"What's her alibi?"

Was she flying in her invisible jet?

Pierce turned in his seat to face me. "She was wallpapering James McKellan's apartment."

Chapter 25

Paninis and Pouty Faces

After Pierce and I talked for a while in his car, I promised him I would stay out of the case, then climbed into my Trailblazer and drove to a deli for a sandwich and to think about what we'd learned.

I ordered a ham, turkey, cheese panini, and a side of sweet potato fries, grabbed a bottle of water from the self-serve cooler and plopped down on a stool near the window.

Sally was wallpapering James' apartment at the time of Eben's murder. Why Sally? Had she offered to do it, or had Miranda set it up? Did James know that Sally was involved with Eben?

The day I'd seen James hugging Miranda, was that a clue that they were closer than I realized? A little niggling thought reared its head. What if James is somehow involved in both murders? What if, indirectly, he orchestrated both? It wasn't inconceivable. Charles Manson had orchestrated a killing spree. I shook my head.

Our sweet pharmacist was no Manson.

I promised Pierce I would stop, but what could it hurt if I drove by James' place and asked him about Sally? There was probably a reasonable explanation for how James was connected to the woman.

I finished my food, then drove over to James' apartment. I rang the doorbell, then knocked when he didn't answer immediately. Still no answer. I poked my head around to the parking lot, scanning it for James' car. It wasn't here.

Disappointment flooded me as I made my way back to my vehicle. I really wanted to know how it happened to be that James had Sally wallpapering his place. Why her? I sat in my car for a minute, tapping the steering wheel. Should I run by Miranda's to see if he was there?

That was a ridiculous idea. Why would he be there? More than likely, he was off doing whatever pharmacists do on their days off when they don't have children. He was probably running errands or golfing.

But, of course, my assumption was purely based on what my dad would do now that I was grown and out of the house.

As I turned off James' street, an idea hit me. What if James had gone to Lydia's house? He was still paying for it, wasn't he? Maybe he planned to sell it. Or move back in. I pulled into the nearest driveway and did a three-point turn. I headed in the opposite direction. If James wasn't at Lydia's, then no harm, no foul.

But if he was?

I might get some answers.

I approached the split-level home and eyed James' car in the driveway. I was elated that I'd been right. Well, at least he wasn't trying to hide his presence. That had to speak volumes about his innocence.

I glanced at Mr. Padasky's house as I walked to the front door. The older man was sitting on his front porch rocker, watching me. I waved.

He waved back.

Stepping up on the front porch, I rang the doorbell. A minute ticked by before a surprised James opened the door. "Kay?"

"Hey, James. I was hoping I would catch you here. Are you busy?"

James looked behind him for a second as if trying to decide whether he was busy. It was strange behavior for him.

When he didn't answer immediately, I continued, "I guess the police don't have this marked as a crime scene anymore, huh?"

"Um, no. They said I could come by and pick up some things if I wanted." His eyes shifted again, and he glanced over his shoulder. Why was he so nervous?

"James, is everything all right?"

His gaze immediately snapped to mine. "Yeah, Kay. You just caught me at a bad time."

"Oh, well-" I started, but another voice cut over mine.

"Ole James has himself a girl in there," Mr. Padasky's voice sounded from behind me. He must have walked over while I was talking to James. James, being so nervous, hadn't noticed him either.

James suddenly appeared flustered. "No, Mr. Padasky, I don't think you've got that right."

"Oh, yes, I do! Boy, I saw her." He turned to me. "Pretty young thing. Dark hair. And tall."

"Tall?" I echoed.

Mr. Padasky held his hand up above my head. "Tall."

I turned to James again. "As in Sally French tall?"

James' face paled. "Kay, I can explain."

Suddenly, a manicured hand reached around the door and pulled it wider. There stood Sally French with a smirk on her pouty face.

Chapter 26

Wallpaper and Chill?

I stared at Sally for a few too many heartbeats, the gears in my head coming to a screeching halt. Sally and James were together at Lydia's place. The gears began slowly churning, trying to make sense of it.

Mr. Padasky let out a low whistle. "Wow, tradin' up, boy."

James shifted his gaze toward Sally, but she stared holes through me.

"What do you want, Kay Wellington?" she asked, ignoring Mr. Padasky's comment.

"Just trying to figure out why you and James are hanging out. When did this start?" I directed my question at James. "Awfully convenient. Sally was secretly dating Eben, and they planned to run off together, but Lydia was in the way. Now Lydia is dead, and Eben is too. You had access to the warfarin in the pharmacy. You have everything to gain from Lydia's death. Pierce was right."

I turned on my heel and slid past Mr. Padasky, who wore a stunned expression on his face.

"No! No, Kay, you're wrong!" James hurried after me as I practically sprinted down the walk. "Hear me out!" He grabbed my arm, then jumped in front of me, blocking my path. I stared him down.

"It's not like that," James whispered loudly, glancing back at Sally, who joined Mr. Padasky on the front porch. The older man was still looking Sally up and down.

"What's it like, James? Did you know that Eben was seeing Sally behind Lydia's back? How did she come to "wallpaper" your apartment?" I used air quotes because I had no idea if wallpaper meant actual wallpaper to Sally at this point.

James looked confused. "Wallpaper?"

I rolled my eyes. "Sally told Detective Cornell that she couldn't have killed Eben because she was wallpapering your apartment. Maybe the two of you should get your stories straight." I tried to move past him, but James tightened his grip on my arm. Something akin to a red flag went off in my head.

"Let go of my arm, James."

"Not until you hear me out." Something in James' eyes shifted. He looked...desperate. "Come inside the house. I'll tell you everything."

I studied James' face. There was something I'd never seen before, and I wasn't sure what it was. Almost like a hardness. But that had to be ridiculous. I'd known the man for years. He was always the calm and collected guy, the reliable guy. He was safe.

I glanced over to the porch where Sally stood texting on her phone with one hand.

"You'll explain everything to me?"

"I promise. When I'm done, you won't have any more questions."

The siren in my head blew. Did James really have something to do with the murders? Was Sally in on it? Was Miranda involved? If I walked in there with them, would I ever come out?

"Mr. Padasky? Will you accompany me inside the house to hear James' story?"

"Kay," James started, but I put my hand up.

"Just trying to be careful, James. Either Mr. Padasky goes inside with me, or I call Detective Cornell, and he can join us."

James' eyes glittered for a second, again with an uncertain emotion. "You seem different, Kay. More...disagreeable."

"Disagreeable? Why? Because I suspect you and Sally might have done something horrible to two people?"

This time, James jerked me closer to him. The sudden movement surprised me as I hit his chest hard. His mouth came close to my ear. "Come inside the house quietly, or something horrible *will* happen to Mr. Padasky."

James' eyes told me he was being honest, maybe for the first time, if his behavior was any indication. My eyes teared up as I peered over at a bewildered Mr. Padasky. He was still on the front porch watching us, but Sally was standing slightly behind him. Something flashed in her hand.

Sally held a knife.

Chapter 27

Three's a Crowd, Four's Just Weird

"O kay," I whispered to James. "Just don't do anything you'll regret later."

"Come inside, and I'll explain everything to you," he breathed close to my ear again. Although James wasn't as tall as Pierce, he felt solid. And in excellent shape. There was no way I could outrun him.

"What are you going to do?" I asked.

He didn't answer as I allowed him to lead me up the walk toward the house. Sally stood near Mr. Padasky, one hand holding her cell and the other clutching a knife. Had she had the knife behind her back when she'd opened the door?

"Nothing to Mr. Padasky if you cooperate. Please, Kay. I'm begging you." His calm voice sounded like James'. But the man pulling me by my arm didn't seem like him at all.

As we neared the porch, Mr. Padasky frowned. "I think I should join you, Kay. I could use a visit."

"Now's not a good time, Mr. Padasky," James answered for me. "I need to talk with Kay about something privately."

"Oh? Like what?"

Mr. Padasky was not going to let this go. I saw Sally and James exchange glances. She still held the knife at an angle near the older man's kidneys. She narrowed her eyes at me.

I sighed. "It has to do with the pharmacy. Something we don't want Dad to know about."

Mr. Padasky made a hmph sound. "Somethin' to do with Lydia' gettin' the wrong medicine?"

Crap. He was quick.

"Maybe. Kay's not perfect all the time," James answered.

I stared at the man I thought had been my coworker and friend. He was implying that I had switched Lydia's medicine from Claritin to Coumadin, knowing the warfarin being an anticoagulant, would cause her blood to thin, leading to dizziness and possibly internal bleeding.

But aside from that blatant lie, I couldn't let Sally hurt poor Mr. Padasky. "It's okay, Mr. Padasky. I'll be fine."

"You sure, Kay?" Mr. Padasky asked me, but his dull eyes were studying James. "I'm supposed to have coffee with that detective fella, but I can hold him off."

Pierce? Mr. Padasky was supposed to have coffee with Pierce?!

My stomach fluttered and then landed with a sick thud. Pierce didn't know I was here. Even if Mr. Padasky told him, Pierce would think I was talking to James. He would never know I was in danger.

"You're having coffee with Detective Cornell?" Sally suddenly asked, moving the knife behind her and out of the older man's view as he turned.

"Yep. That boy and I have become friends." He turned back to James. "You'd like him, James. Cares an awful lot about Kay here. Maybe I can send him over to visit?"

James sucked in a breath.

I took the opportunity to nudge James with my shoulder. He locked gazes with me as I whispered, "If you don't let me leave, he will send Detective Cornell here to see me.

James squeezed his eyes shut. "It's not what you think, Kay. I don't have much-"

"I've had enough," Sally interrupted, raising her voice. "Mr. Padasky, sure, you can come inside. If you're that nosy, then you might as well join us."

Mr. Padasky frowned at James. "Gotcha yourself another rude one, James. In my day, we called that a red flag."

James didn't answer as he tugged me up the porch steps and into the house behind Sally, who motioned for me to go on up to the living room. Mr. Padasky slowly ascended the steps with his cane.

I glanced around the room. There had to be something I could use to defend myself and Mr. Padasky. But what would I do with James even if I knocked the knife away from Sally?

"James, sit! You're making me nervous," Sally barked. James sighed and eased himself onto the couch, pulling me down with him.

"Don't do anything to them, Sally. They're innocent. Especially the old man."

"Old man!" Mr. Padasky practically yelled as he lowered himself onto a nearby recliner. "Boy, I fought in wars. I may be older, but I am not an old man."

James, undeterred, continued, "You got what you wanted, Sally. What you all wanted. Why don't you leave us alone?"

Sally revealed the knife from behind her back and waved it toward James. "What *I* want? How did I get what I wanted? It's *never* been about my wants."

"Why's your girl wielding a knife, James?" Mr. Padasky asked, watching the gorgeous woman wave it around like slicing an invisible tomato.

"I'm *not* his girl. I was Eben's." Her voice caught in her throat for a fraction of a second, but then she recovered. "But Eben wanted it all. He was never content with just me. He wanted what Lydia could offer him." She narrowed her crazy eyes at me and added, "And apparently, you."

I threw my hands up. "No, no. Not me. Nothing was going on between Eben and me."

"But you said-"

"I made it up. To see your reaction, Sally. That's all. Eben and I barely spoke, and when we did, it was about Lydia."

Sally let out a chuckle. "Like I'm going to believe that. My dad told me he saw the two of you."

"He thought he saw something, but it was only Eben leaning over me. I swear."

"Why should I believe you?"

"Sally," James' voice growled. He seemed annoyed with the conversation. "What are you going to do? It's not too late. Mr. Padasky and Kay don't have anything to do with this."

She studied him for a moment. "I don't know. They're on their way here now."

"Who?" Mr. Padasky and I asked in unison.

James exhaled. "Sally, call them off. It's not too late. What will you do when the police detective shows up next door to see Mr. Padasky, and he doesn't answer the door?"

Sally blinked a few times, then shrugged. "He'll just leave."

"Not when he sees Kay's car parked out front of this house. He will walk over here to check on her."

Sally swallowed. I was sure she was going over the situation and the repercussions.

The doorbell rang, and an expletive came out of James' mouth. He looked as scared as I felt.

Sally raised her chin. "It doesn't matter now. They're here. They'll know what to do with all three of you."

Chapter 28

A Family Who Slays Together

"James? Who's here?" I whispered as Sally left us to go down the stairs to answer the front door.

James pulled me closer to him, almost protectively, his wild eyes darting around the room. "I have to get you to safety. Can you run to the backdoor?"

The backdoor was in the kitchen. I would need to run through the living and dining rooms to get to the kitchen.

"Maybe."

I heard voices as Sally opened the door. James jumped up, pulling me back up with him. "Go, now. Run as fast as you can. I'll stall them." He pushed me away, his eyes on the railing, waiting for someone to climb the stairs.

I didn't waste any time. I hated leaving Mr. Padasky, but if I could get help, we would return for him... and James. At least, I was kind of confident that James was on my side. I sprinted through the dining room and into the kitchen. I could hear Sally's voice in the living room and a retort from James. My hand wrapped around the doorknob to the back door, and I turned it, throwing the door open.

I started out when a big hand wrapped around my throat and pushed me against the side of the house.

"Kay Wellington! What a nice surprise."

Mr. French pulled me close to his face, his curled-up mustache hiding his snarl.

"A nice surprise indeed." His breath reminded me of onion ring chips. I twisted in his grip, but he had me. He was already lugging me back into the house, his hand still around my throat and his other arm around my waist.

"Sally! Shut this door and lock it!"

Sally came running through the house, her eyes wide. Fear wound through me. Sally and her father were in this together. They had killed Lydia and Eben and now wanted to kill me.

But why?

"Why are you doing this?" I choked out, trying to twist my body so the big man would have to set me down.

He dropped me on the living room floor, my shoulder slamming hard against the carpet. James quickly grabbed me and helped me to the cushion beside him on the couch. I glanced at Mr. Padasky. He had his eyes glued on Mrs. French, who held a gun in her hand as she stood at the top of the stairs.

It's all three of them.

"Why are you doing this? What do you want?" I asked again, rubbing my throat.

How are we going to get out of this?

"This isn't what I wanted, Kay," Mrs. French answered. "I just wanted to see if your lover had told you anything about us. About what we do. He told Lydia."

"Eben? You're talking about Eben. Eben and I were never together. But he did tell Lydia something, didn't he?"

The woman scrunched her face up. "That hideous woman thought she could blackmail us. Us! Have you any idea who we are? She was a stupid woman. I told Eben that."

"What business do you do?" Mr. Padasky asked, leaning his chin on his cane like watching a movie. "I don't think you would have killed the woman over some groceries."

Mr. French made a clucking sound with his tongue. "You shouldn't even be here. Why is he here?" He directed the question to Sally.

Sally, who stood quietly in the corner with her arms across her chest, shrugged. "He walked over when Kay arrived. So what was I supposed to do? He said he's to meet with Detective Cornell in a bit."

That made Mr. French turn back to the older man. "Is that so?"

"So what business are you into that made Lydia a liability?" I asked. Maybe if I stalled long enough, Pierce would come over to the house once he realized that Mr. Padasky wasn't answering his door.

"We manage the importation of goods and services," Mrs. French said calmly.

"Like diamonds and drugs?"

Her glare bore into mine. "Among other things."

I spun on James beside me. "So what? *You* helped them?"

"Not like that," he answered, his eyes darting again between the Frenchs and me. "I would've never hurt Lydia. Mr. French came into the pharmacy one day and told me he was out of warfarin. He said his usual pharmacy was closed and asked if I could fill a prescription for him. I asked him for the bottle, but he said he didn't have it. I know it was wrong, but I thought he would be a new customer. So I created a fake prescription for him. I dispensed the warfarin to him."

My mouth dropped open. "The warfarin that was given to Lydia."

"It would have worked too, been nice and clean, except that someone is extraordinarily jealous." Mrs. French looked over at her daughter.

"You killed Lydia?" I asked Sally.

Sally swallowed hard. "She didn't give me a choice. She was a horrible woman. I came over here to confront her about my tennis bracelet, and she laughed in my face. Told me to remind my folks that she held the cards. She could have all the diamonds she wanted. All the blood diamonds." Sally blinked a few times. "I hadn't planned on hurting her. She was walking away, and I followed her down the stairs. She said something else about Eben being hers, and I snapped. I grabbed her by the hair and slammed her head into the newel post. It didn't kill her right away. She bounced away from me, slurring her words. Then she dropped onto the floor of the family room. That's when I realized she was dead. Blood pooled around her head, and her eyes were open."

James reached over and squeezed my hand. "That's when the Frenchs told me I needed to do what they said, or they would make sure I went down for her murder."

"And Eben?" I asked quietly to no one particular in the room.

"That boy was worthless. He was a leak. He was the reason Lydia found out. I'm still not convinced he didn't let something slip to Regan, Lydia's sister. He was often seen in her company." Mrs. French raised the gun at me. "And, of course, he may have told you."

"If I'd known, I would have gone to the police," I blurted out. *Crap.*

Why couldn't I be quiet Kay right now? Because my life is in danger, I need to stall or think of a way out of this.

Mr. Padasky slammed the tip of his cane down onto the carpet. The thud made us all jump. "I need to pee," he announced, not the least bit perplexed that our lives hung in the balance.

"We don't have time, old man," Mr. French sneered.

"If I don't go soon, there's going to be a mess. Who wants to smell urine for the rest of the day? Think you can transport me somewhere without gettin' pee on yourself? Maybe your wife could carry me?"

Mrs. French and Sally both made a disgusted sound.

"All right! Get up then and go! There's a bathroom right there. Don't try anything that will get everyone killed." Mr. French pointed down the hall to the first door on the right, the guest bathroom.

Mr. Padasky made a show of getting up, griping, and groaning the whole time. I wondered if I should help, then reminded myself that the man was capable of using the restroom on his own. Mr. Padasky seemed wobbly, however, and tipped forward for a second. I jumped up to catch him, but he righted himself before headbutting me. His dried lips scraped against my cheek. He whispered something before winking at me and hobbling off to the bathroom.

His words echoed through my mind, and dread filled my belly even more as I took in Mr. and Mrs. French's expressions as they quietly discussed what to do with us.

Mr. Padasky had whispered, "Don't worry, girl. We've got this."

Chapter 29

A Last Ditch Effort

"I still can't wrap my head around this," I remarked, pulling the Frenchs' attention from the closed bathroom door where Mr. Padasky had disappeared. Whatever that man was planning might get us killed.

"I mean, you're saying that the three of you are involved in importing and distributing drugs and stolen jewelry? I guess the grocery store is just a front? How did Eben get involved?"

"What are you? Wearing a wire?" Mr. French started toward me, and I shrank back. James jumped up, although he seemed pin thin compared to the black-mustached villain.

"Leave her alone! She's just trying to make sense of this. You owe us an explanation."

"I don't owe you anything!" the man snarled.

But Mrs. French stepped forward and touched her husband's forearm. "Eben was a sly one. First, he got nosy and started looking in boxes in the back of the store. Then, one day, he approached us in the office and said he could help us expand our side hustle in Locklyn and Charlotte. He promised us he had access to the younger tourists headed to Holden Beach and Myrtle every year. After that, he said he just wanted a slice of the pie." She snorted out a laugh. "I didn't know he meant part of his take would include my daughter."

Sally shifted and looked down at the floor.

"So, that's why you killed him? Because he may have told Lydia something, and he was seeing your daughter...which you did not approve."

"And because he suspected that Sally, or we, had killed Lydia." Mrs. French jutted her chin out. "It was an accident that Sally killed the woman. She hadn't meant to. There was no reason to ruin her life too."

"So what happens now?" James asked.

I stared at Mrs. French, who still held the gun. If I moved fast enough, I might be able to wrestle it away from the woman. But Sally still had the knife. And then there was Mr. French with his brawn.

"You can't shoot us here. A neighbor will hear," I said, hoping they would believe me.

"I know," Mrs. French made a face. I suspected she was the ringleader in this little band of thieves/dealers. "My husband is going to pull our truck around back, and the three of you will go out and get in it. If anyone tries anything, I'll take my chances on the neighbors hearing something. Now stand up!" She stepped backward and used the gun to motion for James and me to rise.

Oh God, what are we to do?

"Where's the old man?" Mrs. French asked. "Go get him, Sally."

Mrs. French motioned again at us to walk toward the back of the house as Sally went to the bathroom door. The girl knocked forcefully on the door.

"Mr. Padasky, let's go!"

It was quiet.

Mr. French put his hand out for us to halt. "Let me." The big man strolled to the door and banged it with his closed fist. "Open up, old man!"

The door suddenly swung open, and Mr. Padasky hit Mr. French with the handle of his cane. The movement surprised the man, and he grabbed for his head as Mr. Padasky landed a second blow.

James ran toward the two men and tackled Mr. French as Sally screamed. Mrs. French held the gun higher. "Enough!" she cried.

I took that as an opportunity, pulled out the can of pepper spray, and let it rip into Mrs. French's eyes. The woman screamed, dropping the gun and clawing at her face.

I grabbed for the gun. I'd never held one before, and it was a little frightening. *What if it went off by accident?*

"Stop!" I yelled.

On the floor, Mr. French and James pushed away from each other. Sally still held the knife, but she seemed ineffectual. Mrs. French was rolling on the floor, crying, and trying to use her shirt to wipe at her eyes.

"Mr. Padasky, get that knife." I nodded toward the weapon in Sally's hand, keeping the gun trained on her father. He was the most significant threat.

The old man seemed out of breath, but he jerked the knife from Sally's hand, then hobbled over to the reclining chair. Reaching into the cushion, he produced a cell phone.

"Is that yours?" I asked. "Can you call the police?"

"Already did, Kay," he answered, then placed it against his face. "You still there, Cornell? We're upstairs." Mr. Padasky glanced at me. "The police are here now. Detective Cornell heard everything."

Mrs. French, who had stopped crying, gasped at the news.

Good. Pierce was here.

"When did you call the police?" James asked.

But before Mr. Padasky could answer, Mrs. French made one last-ditch effort, grabbing for the gun in my hands.

Chapter 30
That's How You Do It

E verything happened in a blur.

Mrs. French wrapped her hands around the gun, tightening and trying to wrench it from my hand. I needed to remove my finger from the trigger, so it wouldn't accidentally go off, but her grip was sure.

I jerked and used my leg as leverage against the thin but impossibly strong woman. Her adrenaline had to be in high gear.

I could hear a commotion in the room, which I assumed was Mr. French and James going at it again.

Mrs. French pulled harder, and we landed on the floor, the gun still between us; the cold metal was heavy. *God, please don't let it go off and kill anyone,* I prayed.

Suddenly, strong arms wrapped around me, pulling me from the floor, and another pair grabbed Mrs. French. A hand bent Mrs. French's wrist. She let go of the gun and howled in pain. The same hand carefully took the gun from me and slid the safety.

I was startled at the sight of Pierce and what appeared to be six uniformed police officers in the room. Two of the cops had pulled Mrs. French and me apart. The others handled Mr. French and Sally, although they were mainly on the big man. He was on the floor, face down, handcuffed.

James was rubbing his shoulder, and I noticed the darkening spots on his face. He'd taken quite a beating to keep Mr. French from getting loose.

Mr. Padasky slammed his hand on James' shoulder, and the pharmacist winced. "That's how you do it, boy! Now you're all grown up."

James gave a small chuckle.

"How did you know?" I asked Pierce. "When did Mr. Padasky call you?"

Pierce nodded toward the older man. "I'd been stopping by, talking to Mr. Padasky about once a day. But today, I got this call from him, with muffled noises and voices. I turned the volume up and realized you three were in trouble. Since the phone was Mr. Padasky's cell, I figured you were at his house or here. I called it in but had to wait until all the officers arrived. We didn't want the sirens to spook the Frenchs."

"What happens now?" James asked, still rubbing his shoulder.

Pierce's eyes grazed over me before he turned his attention back to James. "There's an ambulance outside. I want the three of you checked out, and then we'll take statements. Those three," he added, motioning toward the Frenchs, who were being led away in handcuffs by the officers, "are going straight to jail."

Chapter 31

The Perfect Ending?

Two evenings later, I sat on the veranda of a little restaurant in Shallotte near the Holden Beach Bridge. I sipped my iced tea as I took in the view of the canal. It was beautiful and peaceful here. There was a slight breeze, perfect for the blue sundress I'd decided to wear.

Pierce sat across from me in cargo shorts and an olive green tee that showed off his arms and chest.

"Finally," he said, a grin planted on his face. "I feel like I've spent months trying to get you alone for dinner."

I smiled. "It does feel like that. At least the people responsible for Lydia and Eben's deaths are behind bars."

Pierce sat back. "Well, they're awaiting trial, but I doubt a judge will give them a chance at bail. Not with your testimony and those of Mr. Padasky and James. Plus, everything I heard over the phone."

"Is everyone still insisting that Miranda had nothing to do with it?"

"That's what they say. She denies knowing her best friend killed Lydia."

We were both quiet for a moment.

It was over.

We enjoyed a dinner of lobster and shrimp, courtesy of Pierce. Then he suggested we drive across the bridge and walk along the beach.

The breeze picked up into a wind, and the waves came in strong. I slipped off my sandals to walk at the edge and feel the warm saltwater slip between my toes. Pierce carried his shoes, too but held my hand in his.

This was nice. It felt safe. When Pierce slowed and moved in front of me, I was ready. He bent down and brushed his lips over mine. As his hands encircled my waist, the seagulls called, and I only faintly noticed the sound of children playing further down the beach. As my arms slipped around his neck, the pocket of my sundress vibrated against my thigh.

I sighed and pulled away from the best kiss I'd ever had to answer my cell.

"Sorry. Just a second, Pierce."

Pierce's mouth twitched into a grin, but he didn't let go of my waist.

"Hello?"

"Katherine? Thank God! Are you with Detective Cornell?"

"Mom? Is everything okay?" I glanced up at Pierce. He frowned, studying my face.

"No, Kay. It's not. Your father is missing!"

Thanks for reading Mortar and Pestilence: A Kay Wellington Cozy Mystery. Would you consider leaving a rating and review if you liked the story? It helps to get the story out where others can see it.

Want to know when another Kay Wellington Cozy Mystery will hit the shelves? Sign up for my VIP Newsletter, and you'll be the first to know. You can also type the address at https://landing.mailerlite.com/webforms/landing/t9p8s4

About Author

Melissa Plantz is a Christian author and the founder of FIRE & GRACE Publishing. She writes Christian Supernatural Romantic Thrillers, Clean Carolina Romances with a Splash of Mystery, and Cozy Mysteries.

When not writing, Melissa enjoys spending time with her family, drinking too much coffee, lobbying to make sea salt dark chocolate caramels a food group, and conversing with old and new fictional characters. You can find her living the lake bum life or out enjoying the ocean.

Connect with her at AuthorMelissaPlantz @ fireandgracepublishing.com

Artwork Credit: Kali Woods

Books By Melissa Plantz

Don't forget to check out the other books available on Amazon and
Kindle Unlimited:

The Muladach Series

Book #1 The Muladach

Bonus Scene: Alec

Book #2 The Maddening

Book #2.5 The Seer, Prequel to the Muladach series

Book #3 The Beacon

Book #4 The Covenant

Bonus Scene: Astrid

Other Books by Melissa Plantz

Mortar and Pestilence: A Kay Wellington Cozy Mystery

Fire and Grace: A Young Adult Christian Supernatural Thriller

Take the Realm: 10 Days of Spiritual Battle Plans to Reignite the
Weary Warrior Devotional

Kindle Vella:

Mortar and Pestilence: A Kay Wellington Cozy Mystery

Keeping Our Secrets For All Time (A Clean Time Travel Romance)

To winter weather.

I miss you.